Enid Blyton

STORIES OF
ROTTEN
RASCALS

D1635299

Look out for all of these enchanting story collections

by *Enid Blyton*

Enid Blyton

STORIES OF
ROTTEN
RASCALS

Hodder
Children's
Books

HODDER CHILDREN'S BOOKS

This collection first published in Great Britain in 2020
by Hodder & Stoughton

3 5 7 9 10 8 6 4

Enid Blyton ® and Enid Blyton's signature are registered trade marks
of Hodder & Stoughton Limited
Text © 2020 Hodder & Stoughton Limited
Illustrations © 2020 Hodder & Stoughton Limited

A CIP catalogue record for this book is available from the British Library.

ISBN 978 1 444 95427 2

Printed and bound in Great Britain by Clays Ltd, Elcograf S.p.A.

The paper and board used in this book are made from
wood from responsible sources.

Hodder Children's Books
An imprint of Hachette Children's Group
Part of Hodder & Stoughton
Carmelite House
50 Victoria Embankment
London EC4Y 0DZ

An Hachette UK Company
www.hachette.co.uk
www.hachettechildrens.co.uk

Contents

Untidy William

Untidy William

THERE WAS once a boy who was very untidy. His name was William, and his mother was always scolding him for being so untidy.

'You never put *any*thing away, William!' she would say. 'You leave your shoes out – you leave your cap on the floor – you throw your coat down. It's simply dreadful.'

'Sorry, Mother!' said William cheerfully.

'You're *not* sorry!' said his mother. 'If you were, you would try to do better. I am always clearing up after you – and yet you never try to help me.'

'Well, I *will* try!' said William. So the next day he

really tried. He hung up his cap on the peg, and he put his shoes into the cupboard. Gracious, he did feel good! But as he dropped his coat on the floor and left his scarf on the stairs, he didn't really do very well after all!

He went upstairs. He opened the desk he had there to find a favourite pencil. He couldn't find it, so he scrabbled about in the desk just as if he were a dog scratching in the ground for a hidden bone – and, of course, everything went flying out of his desk on to the floor!

Did William pick them up? Of course not! Hadn't he hung up his cap on the peg and put his shoes away in the cupboard? Well, that was tidiness enough for one day, as far as William was concerned.

Then William sat down on the clean bedcover and creased that. He knocked his pyjamas on to the floor and didn't pick them up. His mother came in to speak to him and saw the untidy mess in his bedroom.

'William I thought you were going to try and be really tidy today!' she said. 'And you seem to be worse than ever!'

'Well, Mother, I like that!' said William. 'Didn't you see how I had hung up my cap on its peg, and put my shoes away in the cupboard? I do think you might have noticed that!'

'All I noticed was that your coat was on the floor in the hall, and I tripped over your scarf as I came upstairs!' said his mother. 'William, I don't know what to do with you.'

She went out of the room. William sat and thought for a minute. Then he got up.

I've often read in stories that people can get spells from the fairy folk to put things right when they are untidy and untruthful or greedy, he thought. *I've a good mind to go to old Dame Goody and ask her if she knows of one to keep me tidy. Then I wouldn't keep getting into trouble with Mother. It would be so nice to be tidy without having to keep on remembering it.*

He put on his outdoor things and went up the hill to where old Dame Goody lived. She was a funny little old lady, and she had most peculiar eyes. Sometimes they looked grey and sometimes they looked green. That was because her grandmother had been first cousin to a fairy.

Well, Dame Goody was surprised to see William, for usually the children were rather afraid of her, though she was a kind old lady who wouldn't have hurt anybody for anything.

'Good morning, Dame Goody,' said William. 'I expect you know that I'm awfully untidy, don't you?'

'Well, I can see it,' said the old woman, looking down at William's shoes, which were both undone, and at his coat, which had the buttons done up wrongly.

'Do you think you could possibly give me a spell to make me tidy without my bothering much about it?' asked William. 'I would so much like one. I could pay you for it. I've got a shilling in my moneybox.'

'Well, I believe I *have* got an old, old spell tucked away somewhere that my grandmother had by her,' said Dame Goody, her eyes suddenly looking very green. 'And if it would do for a tidy spell, you can have it for a shilling.'

She went off into the back room, and William heard her hunting in drawers for the old, old spell. At last she came back, smiling. She held a funny little tin in her hand. It was bright blue, and at the top it had a head instead of a lid.

'I've found the spell,' said Dame Goody. 'I'll scatter it over you, and you will then find that your things will all be terribly tidy!'

'But *I* want to be tidy,' said William, 'not my things.'

'Well, it's easier to make your things tidy than you,' said Dame Goody. 'Now stand still, please!'

William stood still. Dame Goody took off the funny little wooden head that was on the top of the tin instead of a lid, and scattered a blue powder all over William.

'I feel as if you are peppering me!' said William, beginning to sneeze. '*A-tish-oo!*'

Dame Goody muttered a string of magic words that sounded very strange to William. Then she clapped the lid on to the tin, and nodded her head at him.

'The spell will work tomorrow morning,' she said. 'I hope it's all right. It's rather old, you see. It may have gone a bit wrong.'

'What should it do?' asked William.

'Well, it should make anything belonging to you put itself neatly away,' said Dame Goody. 'Your pencils should put themselves away in the box. Your cap should hang itself up on the peg. Your clothes should fold themselves up neatly when you take them off, and put themselves on a chair or away in a drawer.'

'That sounds marvellous!' said William, pleased. 'Thank you, Dame Goody. I shall now be known as the tidiest boy in the country!' He went off, smiling, wishing that the next day would come quickly.

It came. William awoke, dressed himself, and then threw down his pyjamas on the floor on purpose to see if the spell was working.

And do you know, those pyjamas solemnly got up, folded themselves neatly and put themselves into the pyjama case on the bed. It was most extraordinary to watch them.

This is great! thought William. *Simply great!*

He threw his toothbrush on to the floor. It at once flew up into the air, and settled itself calmly into the tooth mug. William was very pleased indeed.

He went downstairs, in good time for breakfast. His father was there, reading the newspaper, and he looked up as William came in. 'Hallo, son,' he said, and then buried himself behind the paper again.

'Sit down and get on with your porridge,' his mother called from the kitchen. 'I'm just getting the bacon and eggs!'

William sat down. He was just about to put sugar

on his porridge, when something most peculiar happened. His shoes came off, and his socks unpeeled from his legs!

William looked down in astonishment. Whatever could be happening? To his enormous surprise he saw his shoes hopping neatly together over the floor. They went out of the door, and he heard them going to the hall cupboard! Well, well, well!

His socks rolled themselves into a neat ball, and then bowled themselves out of the door too. They went upstairs and put themselves into a drawer.

Then William's jacket took itself off William and flew away to hang itself up. His shirt and tie came off and his shorts. They all folded themselves up very neatly indeed, and then went upstairs to put themselves away.

And there was William sitting at the breakfast table in his vest! He simply didn't know what to do.

My goodness! The spell has *gone wrong!* he thought in dismay. *Instead of waiting until I was untidy, my things*

have put themselves away now! I'd better creep upstairs
before anyone sees me and dress again.

Well, William was just about to creep away when
his mother came into the room with the bacon and
eggs. She saw William sitting at the table in his vest
and she almost dropped the dish in amazement.

'William! Why haven't you dressed? Don't you
know that you are only in your vest? Really, is this
the way to come down to breakfast? What in the
world are you thinking of?'

Daddy looked up in surprise. How he stared when
he saw poor William in nothing but his vest!

'Is this a joke?' he asked. 'Because, if so, I don't
think it is at all amusing! Boys who come down in
their vests ought to be punished.'

William fled upstairs. Goodness, this was dreadful!
He didn't like it at all!

William found his things in the drawers and in
his cupboard and dressed himself again. He tied his
shoelaces firmly in a knot, in case his shoes thought of

hopping off again. He did up all his buttons tightly.

It would be simply dreadful if they all came off again, he thought. *I really don't know what Daddy would say!*

Well, nothing happened at breakfast time except that a spoon, which William dropped, hopped up to the table again on its own and put itself neatly by William's plate.

Now that's good, thought William. *That's the sort of thing I wanted the spell for. If only it goes on working like that, it will be fine.*

But it didn't! William put on his cap, jacket, scarf and gloves, and went to catch the bus to go to school. And in the bus, his cap, jacket, scarf and gloves all undid themselves, and sailed away out of the bus door! They fled home, hung themselves up or put themselves in a drawer – and there was poor cold William shivering in the bus without any of his outdoor clothes! There was only an old man in the bus besides William. The conductor was on the top of the bus. The old man was rather astonished to see William without any cap or coat, but he said nothing.

But Mr Brown, his teacher, said quite a lot. 'William! How is it that you have come to school like this? Really, what are you thinking of to come without your cap or jacket? You will catch a dreadful cold on this bitter winter day!'

William couldn't say that his things had flown away by themselves, so he said nothing. He went into his classroom and sat down.

And immediately all the pencils, rubber and pocketknife in his pocket hopped out to the desk and put themselves tidily into his pencil box! Mr Brown heard the noise and looked up.

'Is it really necessary to make all that noise with your pencil box, William?' he asked. William said he was sorry, and glared at his pencils and rubber and knife. His pencil box lid shut down with a snap.

And then the books on William's desk decided that the right place for them was the bookcase! So they took a jump and landed on the bookshelf with a crash. Everyone looked up.

'William! Did *you* throw your books on to the shelf?' asked Mr Brown. 'What *can* be the matter with you today?'

'I didn't throw them,' said William.

'Well, I suppose you will tell me that they jumped there themselves!' said Mr Brown.

'That's just what they did do,' said poor William.

'Any more of this behaviour and you will stay in at the end of the morning,' said Mr Brown sternly.

William looked worried. He did hope that the spell wouldn't work any more that morning! Oh, why had he ever tried to get a tidy spell? It was getting him into great difficulties.

After playtime that morning, the children settled down to a history lesson. Mr Brown was teaching them about the people of long ago. William listened well, for he loved history stories.

And then he felt his right shoe twisting about on

his foot! The spell was beginning to work again. The shoe wanted to take itself home and put itself away into the cupboard. But William had tied the laces very tightly and it couldn't get itself off!

William tried to keep his foot still – but the spell worked very hard, and the shoe twisted about so much that it twisted William's foot with it.

'William! Is it *you* fidgeting?' cried Mr Brown at last. 'Keep your feet still!'

But that was just what William couldn't do! The spell began to work in both shoes, and so both William's feet began to fidget about. Mr Brown was very cross.

'Stand up, William,' he said. 'If you can't *sit* still, perhaps you can stand still!'

So William had to stand for the rest of the history lesson, and he didn't like it at all. His shoes twisted about for a while, then grew tired and stopped.

At the end of the morning came a lesson that William liked very much. It was woodwork. William was making a ship. He had a hammer, screwdriver, chisel, pincers, gimlet and nails of his own. He went with the other boys to get his tools from the woodwork cupboard.

Well, the spell began to work again as soon as William was happily hammering nails into his ship. He put down his tools for a moment and took up his ship to ask Mr Brown if it was all right. And when he came back to his desk, his tools had disappeared!

'Who's taken my tools?' asked William, looking all around. Nobody had! It was very mysterious. Then William wondered if the spell was working again. Perhaps his tools had put themselves away in the box in the woodwork cupboard. So he went to look – and sure enough, there they were! William took them out, while all the boys looked on in astonishment.

'Why did you put them away in the middle of the lesson?' asked Dick.

William didn't answer. He didn't know what to say. He set to work again.

Then he went to look at a submarine that another boy was making, and when he got back to his own work – goodness gracious, his tools had disappeared *again*!

William knew where they were, of course – in the toolbox! So he went to get them again. Mr Brown looked up.

'William! Are you going to spend *all* the lesson in going to the cupboard and back for tools?' he asked.

Poor William! All he could say was, 'Sorry, Mr Brown!' He was quite glad when the lesson came to an end.

Just as the children were lined up to be dismissed at half past twelve, William felt his jacket coming undone. Goodness, were his clothes going to rush off again? No, no – he really couldn't bear it! William clutched his jacket to himself very tightly, and held it there.

'William! Have you got a pain or something?' asked Mr Brown in surprise. 'Really, you are behaving in a funny manner today!'

William was glad to get outside – and only just in time too! His jacket tore itself off him and flew down the road like a mad thing. Then his shoes and socks flew off too. William simply couldn't stop them. He stared in the greatest dismay.

The children shouted with laughter. 'Look! The wind has blown away William's clothes! Oh, how funny!'

Poor old William! By the time he got home he had only his shorts and vest left, and he was very cold indeed. He crept in at the back door, hoping that his mother wouldn't notice him. He slipped upstairs. There, neatly hanging up, was his jacket. Folded tidily in the drawer was his shirt. His socks were rolled up in their drawer. His shoes were side by side by the bed.

I simply can't stand this! thought William in despair.

I'm going to go to old Dame Goody at once and beg her to do something about this dreadful spell.

So he dressed himself again quickly and slipped out of the back door to go to old Dame Goody's. He banged loudly on her door and she opened it in surprise.

'Dame Goody! That spell worked all wrong!' said William. 'It's done the most dreadful things. Please do something about it.'

'Dear me, I'm sorry,' said Dame Goody. 'Well, step inside a moment. I've got a special drink that stops spells from working if they are no longer needed. Now, where did I put it?'

She took what looked like a large-sized medicine bottle from a cupboard and poured out a drink for William. Gracious, it did taste horrid!

'Now, the spell won't work any more as long as you try to be tidy yourself,' said Dame Goody. 'It will only work if you are very untidy again. So I should be careful if I were you, William!'

'Goodness! I shall be the tidiest boy in the world!' said William, and he ran off home.

Well, he *isn't* the tidiest boy in the world, but he's a lot better. I watch him whenever I see him just in case I might suddenly see his tie whisk itself away or his cap fly off home to its peg. It really would be fun to see that, wouldn't it!

She Stamped Her Foot

She Stamped Her Foot

MELANIE HAD a dreadful temper. When she was in a rage she went red in the face, shouted – and then stamped her foot!

'Melanie! Please don't stamp your foot at me!' said her mother crossly. 'No matter what you want, I shan't give it to you if you stamp like that. It's rude.'

Melanie stamped her foot again. It wasn't a bit of good – she was just sent up to bed!

So after that she didn't stamp her foot at her mother any more – only at her friends. They couldn't send her to bed, but they didn't like her at all when she stamped her foot at them.

One afternoon Melanie went to pick blackberries in Farmer Giles's field. She knew where there was a fine hedge of them – and as they were the last of the autumn's feast of blackberries, she meant to have a very nice time!

But she found a little old lady there, picking quickly, and putting the big, juicy blackberries into her basket. Melanie stared in rage.

'I came to pick these blackberries,' she said.

'So did I,' said the old lady, still picking.

'I saw them the other day, and I said to myself that they should be mine and no one else's,' said Melanie, going red in the face.

'How funny! That's just what I said to myself!' said the old lady, still picking hard.

Melanie stared crossly. 'I want those blackberries!' she said.

'So do I,' said the old lady. 'You can share them, can't you?'

'You've picked all the biggest. You're greedy,' said rude Melanie.

'What an unpleasant child you are!' said the old

lady, staring at Melanie out of curious green eyes. Those eyes should have warned Melanie that the old lady was magic, for people with green eyes are not always the same as other folk.

'You're not to talk to me like that!' said Melanie – and she stamped her foot. 'You're not to, you're not to!'

'Don't stamp your foot at me, or you'll be sorry!' said the old lady, and her eyes looked rather fierce. But did Melanie care? Not she!

She lost her temper all in a hurry, and began to shout and stamp. 'I want those blackberries!' (Stamp, stamp!) 'I want those blackberries!' (Stamp, stamp!) 'I want those blackberries!' (Stamp, stamp, *stamp*!)

The old lady looked at Melanie in the greatest surprise. 'My dear little girl,' she said, 'you shouldn't have been a child at all. You should have been a pony! Then you could do all the stamping you please!'

'Give me those blackberries!' shouted Melanie, and she stamped so heavily on the grass that she squashed it flat.

'I don't mind horses stamping at me, but I won't have little girls behaving like this,' said the old woman, and she waved a thin brown hand at Melanie. 'Be a pony! Run away and stamp all you like!'

And then, to Melanie's enormous dismay, she found that she was no longer a little girl, but a small brown pony with a white star on its head! She had four legs and a long tail!

She stamped with her forefoot on the grass, and opened her mouth to shout – but she neighed instead, '*Nay – hay – hay – hay – hay! Nay – hay – hay – hay – hay*!'

'Well, if you want hay, go and get it,' said the old lady, going on with her picking. Melanie was frightened by her horse-voice and ran away round the field. Oh dear, this was dreadful! She was a pony – fancy that, a pony! She couldn't speak like a little girl. She couldn't pick blackberries, for she had no hands. She could still stamp, and she could wave her long tail about – how very, very frightening!

Melanie wanted to go home, so she ran to the

field-gate. But it was shut. Melanie stamped her foot, and the old lady laughed.

'Stamp away! I always love to see a horse stamping with its hoof – it's right for horses to paw the ground! Stamp all you like, little pony, and enjoy yourself!'

But Melanie wasn't enjoying herself one bit. Supposing the farmer came by and put her between the shafts of a trap to take people for rides? Suppose he wanted to ride her? He was such a big, heavy man. And what about her food? Would she have to eat grass?

Melanie put her big pony-head down to nibble the grass to see what it tasted like. It was horrid! She still had the tastes and feelings of a little girl although she had the body of a pony! Whatever was she going to do? Why, oh, why had she stamped at that old woman?

Just then George, John, Lucy and Rob came into the field. 'Look!' cried Rob. 'A new pony! Let's ride him!'

Melanie was full of horror. What – let those children ride on her back? Never! She ran away to a corner of the field, and the children followed.

The pony stamped her foot at them, and the children laughed. 'He's like Melanie!' they cried. 'He stamps his foot just like Melanie!'

Just then the children's mother came along and called them. 'Come out of the field, children. There's no time to play before tea. Come along.'

Tea! Melanie felt hungry. How she wished she could go home to eat cakes and jam too. But what would her mother say if a pony came running into the house?

Still – she would go home. Perhaps her mother would know her even though she was a pony. Melanie cried a few big tears out of her large pony-eyes. She cantered out of the gate that the children had carelessly left open, and went down the lane to her home. The door was open. The pony cantered inside – and there was her mother, laying the tea.

'Good gracious! A horse coming to tea!' said Melanie's mother. 'I never heard of such a thing! Shoo! Shoo! Go out at once!'

Melanie went right into the room and put her big pony-head on her mother's shoulder. Tears ran down her big brown pony-nose.

'Well, look at this!' cried her mother in greatest amazement. 'A pony crying on my shoulder! Poor creature, what's the matter? Now, pony, don't be silly,' said her mother, pushing it away. 'Do you think you're a little dog or something, trying to get on my knee? You'll be borrowing my handkerchief to wipe your eyes next! Dear, dear, I don't understand this! I must be in a dream.'

A voice spoke from the doorway. 'No, you are not in a dream. That is Melanie – but she stamped her foot at me, so I changed her into a pony for a time. Horses may stamp when they please, but not children!'

'Oh, dear, oh, dear!' cried Melanie's mother, putting her arms round the pony's neck. 'Now I understand what this poor pony wants. Old woman, you are magic! Change my little girl to her own shape, please! I am sure she will never, never stamp her foot at you again!'

'Will you ever stamp your foot again, Melanie?' the old lady asked the pony. It shook its big head at once. The old woman waved her hand and – lo and behold! – the pony disappeared, and there was Melanie, looking rather small and scared.

'Goodbye,' the old lady said to her. 'Remember that only horses stamp – so be careful you don't change into one again. You never know!'

She went out with her basket of blackberries. Melanie looked at her mother.

'Don't let me stamp my foot any more!' she wept, glad to find that she didn't neigh this time.

'Well, you must try and remember yourself,' said her mother. 'I can't tell your feet what to do!'

Melanie laughed through her tears. 'I'll try and remember,' she said. 'I don't want to eat grass any more – and you don't want a pony stamping about the kitchen, do you, Mummy?'

All the same I hope I'm there if Melanie ever does stamp her foot again – it would be so surprising to see her change into a pony!

He Was a Bit
Too Quick!

WHENEVER ANY of the three children had a sore throat Mother always made them a cup of blackcurrant tea. It was lovely. She took out a pot of blackcurrant jam, put a big spoonful into a cup, and then poured boiling water on to it. She stirred in some sugar, and when the blackcurrant tea was cooling, it made a really lovely drink.

'It's almost worthwhile having a sore throat to be able to drink a cup of Mother's blackcurrant tea,' said Judy. 'And my throat is *always* better after it. Always.'

'So's mine,' said Jack, and Pat said the same. When

George, their cousin, came to stay with them they told him about the blackcurrant tea too.

'Judy's just had a bad throat, and Mother made her some blackcurrant tea,' said Pat. 'It made her throat *much* better – so Mother gave her another cup of it, and after that her throat was well. It's simply lovely stuff.'

Now, George was an artful boy and very greedy too. He thought that blackcurrant tea made from jam would be a lovely thing to have – much nicer than lemonade. But what a pity to have to wait for a sore throat before he could have any!

And then he suddenly had one of his ideas! He could easily *pretend* he had a sore throat.

If I go around coughing a bit, and saying my throat hurts, Aunt Susan will be sure to give me blackcurrant tea, he thought. So he put on a silly little cough, and looked miserable.

'My throat hurts,' he told the others. They told their mother. She looked at George, and remembered that he had eaten a most enormous dinner and that she had heard him yelling immediately afterwards. He couldn't be ill if he ate like that and certainly he wouldn't yell at the top of his voice if his throat was hurting him so much.

She was used to George and his artful ways. 'I don't think George has much of a sore throat,' she said.

'I should like some blackcurrant tea to make it better,' said George at once, and coughed.

'Well, we'll see how you are after tea,' said his aunt. 'I don't waste my blackcurrant tea on anyone who *hasn't* a bad throat, you know.'

George scowled. Then he made himself cough so much that his throat really began to feel quite sore!

His aunt took no notice, but went out of the room. 'I think your mother's unkind,' said George to Pat.

'She's not,' said Pat at once. 'I expect she's gone to get the blackcurrant jam. You'll find it all ready for you to drink soon.'

George hoped Pat was right. He waited for his

aunt to come back, but she didn't. He went up to his bedroom, took down a book and sulked over it for a long time. Horrid Aunt Susan! His mother always made such a fuss of him if he so much as pricked his finger.

After some time he went downstairs to find the others. They had gone out for a walk. George went into the kitchen, scowling and cross. How horrid everyone was!

But then his face brightened. In the middle of the table was a cup of some purplish stuff – *blackcurrant tea*, thought George. Was it for him? Well, he'd drink it anyhow, whether it was for him or not. It looked lovely!

He tipped up the cup and drank the purple liquid straight off. He put the empty cup down and made a face. Ooh! What a nasty taste! Well, if that was blackcurrant tea *he* certainly didn't want any more! How simply disgusting! However could the others like it so much? It wasn't even sweet.

He decided not to say anything more about his throat at all, in case his aunt offered him some more of that horrible tea. So when the others came home he announced that he was quite well again and ready for a game.

'Is your throat better then?' said Judy in surprise.

'Yes, I drank a cup of your mother's blackcurrant tea and it got quite well,' said George. 'What game shall we play now?'

'Pat doesn't feel very like a game,' said Judy. '*She's* got a sore throat now! It came on when we were out. She's gone to ask Mother for some blackcurrant tea.'

Soon Pat came in with her mother. She held a cup full of purplish stuff in her hand. George shuddered. He looked at his aunt. She carried a cup too.

'Here you are, George,' she said, holding it out to him. 'Drink this. You asked me for it before. It will be good for your throat.'

'No thank you, Aunt Susan,' said George. 'I've

already had one cup of blackcurrant tea, and it's made my throat *quite* better!'

His aunt stared at him in surprise. 'Who gave you the tea? I haven't made any till now.'

'I found a cup of it on the table there,' said George. 'It was delicious, Aunt Susan. I drank it all up – and my throat's better.'

To his surprise, Judy, Jack and Pat suddenly began to scream with laughter. Mother was surprised too.

'Oh, dear, what *do* you think George has done?' cried Judy at last. 'We painted in our painting books this afternoon, and when we went out we cleared up except for the paint water. We left it in a cup on the table – and George must have thought it was blackcurrant tea and drank it up! Oh, *George*!'

George went scarlet. His aunt laughed and laughed, and the others clutched each other and roared helplessly.

'He drank our dirty painting water.'

'Was it lovely, George?'

'Have some more?'

'Well, George,' said his aunt, 'I'm very, very glad to hear that you've cured your bad throat with a dose of painting water. How clever of you! I shall know what to give you next time you have a bad throat.'

So now poor George never dares to say he has a cold just in case his aunt remembers what she said and gives him painting water to drink. Well, he shouldn't have pretended, should he?

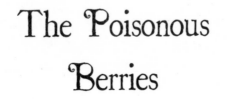

The Poisonous Berries

The Poisonous Berries

'LET'S GO for a walk and see if the nuts are getting ripe!' said Harry.

'Yes, let's,' said Jane. 'We'll get Anna and Jack too, and perhaps George will come if he's done his work.'

'Are you going out?' called Mother. 'Well, now, be careful not to eat any berries that you don't know. You're safe with blackberries and bilberries – but no others, mind!'

'Mother does fuss over us,' said Harry impatiently. 'We should know by the taste if any berries weren't good for us! Hi, Anna! Hi, Jack! Coming for a walk to see if there are any nuts ripe yet?'

'Yes, rather!' cried Jack. 'George! Have you finished your homework? Come along too.'

So the five children went for a good long walk to the woods. By the time they got there they were hungry.

'Ooh! I could eat about a hundred nuts!' said Jack. 'I do hope we find some.'

'There ought to be some blackberries too,' said Jane, looking all about. 'But I think heaps of people must have been here before us – there's not a single berry to be seen!'

'And we couldn't find a single bilberry either, as we came across the common,' said George. 'Well, let's hope there are some nuts. Oh, look! There's a big cluster up there in that hazel tree!'

But alas! Not one of the green nuts was ripe. It was too early in the autumn for them. The children were disappointed.

'I do wish we'd brought some chocolate or something with us,' said Harry. 'I really am hungry.'

'Look! Don't those berries look gorgeous!' cried Jane, suddenly pointing to some brilliant red berries growing on a small plant in a wet ditch. 'Shall we taste them?'

'Of course not,' said Anna at once. 'You know what our mothers say – we must never eat strange berries.'

'Well, I don't see that a taste would do any harm,' said George. 'I'm jolly hungry. If they taste sweet and good they'll be all right.'

'Let's taste them,' said Harry.

'I think you're very silly,' said Anna.

'Old prim and proper!' said Jane laughing. 'You needn't have any!'

The children picked the berries and put them into their mouths. Jack spat his out at once.

'Don't like it,' he said.

George rolled his round his tongue and then spat it out too. 'Not sweet enough for me,' he said.

Harry tried to swallow his, choked and spat it

out. 'It doesn't taste too good,' he said. 'Spit yours out, Jane.'

But Jane wouldn't. She was always more daring than the rest. 'It's nice!' she said. 'Lovely and juicy! I'll have one or two more.'

'You're silly,' said Anna. 'I shall tell your mother. You're being dangerous.'

'Tell-tale! Tell-tale!' shouted everyone, dancing round Anna. She went very red.

'I don't care,' she said. 'There are times when tales have to be told – when it's only sensible to tell them. Suppose Jane gets ill and nobody knows what's the matter with her? Wouldn't you all be glad if I'd told her mother and she knew how to make her better then?'

'I shan't be ill!' said Jane, dancing about, chewing the berries. 'You're an old fusspot!'

But, do you know, long before they got home, Jane began to feel rather ill. Her face went white and she felt sick. She didn't say a word to the others.

She didn't want Anna to say 'I told you so!'

She ran indoors when she got home, and went up to her bedroom. She really felt very sick indeed. But she wasn't going to tell Mother. She just wouldn't!

But Anna did. She went into the kitchen, where Jane's mother was ironing some clothes, and spoke to her.

'Please, Mrs Brown,' she said. 'I don't think Jane is very well. She looked very white when she was coming home.'

'Oh, dear!' said Jane's mother in alarm. 'What do you think is the matter with her?'

'Will you think I am telling tales if I tell you?' asked Anna.

'Of course not, if it is something to do with Jane not being well,' said Mrs Brown. 'It would be only sensible to tell me!'

'Well, Mrs Brown, Jane ate some bright red berries out of the ditch,' said Anna. 'I'm afraid they were poisonous!'

'Thank you for telling me!' cried Mrs Brown and she rushed upstairs to find Jane.

Jane was very ill. Her mother put her to bed, and called the doctor. When he had heard that she had eaten poisonous berries he was worried. He gave her a very nasty drink that made her sick.

'Maybe that will get rid of the poison,' he said. Jane ached and cried, and didn't want anything to eat at all for two days.

The other children were frightened. 'We ought to have taken Anna's advice,' they said. 'We called her an old fusspot – but she was right.'

'And my mother says that if she hadn't been sensible enough to go and tell Mrs Brown at once that Jane had eaten strange berries, Jane might have been much worse than she was,' said George. 'But Mrs Brown was able to call in the doctor at once.'

'Well, there's one thing I've made up *my* mind about!' said Jack. 'And that is – I shall never eat any berries I don't know in future!'

Jane got better in four days. She still looked rather white when she came downstairs. She was pleased to see Anna when she called with some barley sugar for her.

'Anna,' said Jane, 'I'm *so* glad you told tales about me to my mother! You were the only sensible one of the lot!'

'Well, don't eat poisonous berries any more, or I'll have to tell tales of you again!' laughed Anna.

You won't either, will you? And if there are any of your friends who are silly about berries, just lend them this story. They'll be careful after that!

Billy Bitten-Nails

Billy Bitten-Nails

BILLY BROWN had such a funny name at school – he was called Billy Bitten-Nails! I expect you can guess why! He bit his nails very badly, and they looked dreadfully ugly.

His mother asked him not to bite them. His teacher told him how horrid they looked. His friends laughed at him and said, 'His nails must taste nice because he always seemed to be eating them.' But nothing that anyone said made any difference to Billy Bitten-Nails. He just went on biting them.

Now one day Billy did a good turn for the pixies. He happened to be going through the woods when he heard somebody making such a fuss.

'Look at that!' cried a little high voice. 'Right up in the tree, where I can't possibly reach it! It's too bad of the goblins to play a trick like that on me. I can't possibly get it again – it's much too high in the tree!'

Then Billy heard other little voices, and he peeped round the tree to see what all the fuss was about, and to his great surprise he saw three small pixies looking up into a prickly holly tree!

'Hallo!' said Billy. 'What's the matter? What is up in the tree?'

'My best hat,' said one of the pixies. 'The goblins came along a few minutes ago, snatched my hat off my head and threw it up into the tree. I can't get it because it's too high up, and the tree is terribly prickly.'

'Well, I'll get it for you,' said Billy, picking up a stone. 'I can aim very well. I'll knock your hat out of the tree in a twinkling! Stand away or the stone may hit you.'

Billy threw the stone hard at the hat. It hit it –

bang! The hat fell down out of the tree, almost on to the waiting pixie's head. He gave a squeak of delight and caught it.

'Thank you, you kind boy!' said the little fellow. 'It's so good of you to help me. I'll do something for you in return. Now, let me look at you – I wonder what you'd like me to do!'

The tiny pixie stared hard at Billy from his head to his feet, and suddenly he saw Billy's bitten nails. He smiled and nodded his gay little head.

'Ah!' he said. 'I see you hate your nails! You are trying to bite them all away. I will help you! If you don't want your nails you needn't have any!'

Before Billy could say anything the little pixie touched all his nails one after the other with his own tiny fingers. As he touched them he said such a magic word that Billy trembled. He had never heard a magic word before and it had a very strange and curious sound.

'There you are!' cried the pixie in delight. 'You

won't have to bite your nails away any more! They are gone!'

Billy looked down at his hands – and how he stared! All his nails were gone! Yes, really. His fingers were very queer-looking indeed – just fingers right to the top without any nails at all. Whatever would everyone say?

'Oh, please, I don't like this,' he began – and then he stopped. The pixies had vanished! Not a sign of them was to be seen. And there was poor old Billy, with no nails on his fingers. He put his hands into his pockets and walked off home, feeling most alarmed.

He kept his hands in his pockets all that afternoon and, as Mother was out to tea, he had it alone, and no one noticed how queer his fingers looked as he spread his jam and cut his cake. Poor Billy! He couldn't scratch his knees where his shorts rubbed against them, because he hadn't any nails. He couldn't scrape the earth off his sleeve where he had fallen into the mud, because he hadn't any nails to do it with! He couldn't even open his pocketknife as usual, because he hadn't even a bitten nail left to open it with!

'This is simply dreadful!' said Billy to himself. 'Whatever am I to do? I miss my nails terribly. And how shall I explain at school what has happened?'

Well, you should have seen his mother's face when at last she saw that Billy had no nails! She simply couldn't believe it! And when Billy told her what had happened she grew quite pale.

'Oh, dear! I wonder if this means that your nails will never grow again,' she said. 'Your fingers do look so horrid, Billy. I can't imagine what your teacher will say.'

Well, his teacher said quite a lot, and so did the boys and girls.

'I don't know which is the more horrid of the two, Billy,' said his teacher, 'to have bitten nails, or to have no nails at all. You are a most unfortunate little boy. First you make your own fingers ugly, and then the pixies make them even uglier! Well, you must do the best you can without nails. You must get the other children to open your pocketknife for you when you want to sharpen your pencils.'

Billy didn't say anything. He wished and wished that he had never in his life bitten his nails! It was very bad luck that just when he had seen and helped the pixies for the first time, the reward they had given him was something he didn't want.

I'll go through the woods again and call the pixies, thought Billy to himself. *Perhaps they will give me my nails back again.*

So he went. He stood beneath the big holly tree and called loudly, 'Pixies! Pixies! It is Billy calling you. I want you!'

Up ran the tiny pixie whose hat he had got from the tree. 'Hallo, Billy!' he said. 'What's the matter?'

'It's my nails,' said Billy. 'I want them back.'

'But why?' asked the pixie in surprise. 'You had tried to bite them right away. If you don't like your nails it would be silly to have them again.'

'I *do* like my nails,' said Billy. 'It was a silly habit I got into. Please give them back to me.'

'Well,' said the pixie, 'I can make them begin to grow again, Billy, but I'm afraid they won't be quite the same sort of nails that you had before. If you bite them they will squeal out, because they will be magic nails. You will hurt them if you bite them.'

'Well, I won't bite them,' said Billy. 'Please make them grow again.'

The pixie took a small twig growing nearby and touched the tips of Billy's fingers with it, saying another magic word, even stranger than the first he had used. Billy looked at his fingers. He saw that tiny nails were just beginning to grow! Good!

'They will take a few days to get to the tips of your fingers,' said the pixie. 'I'm sorry I did something you didn't like, Billy. Goodbye!'

He disappeared, and Billy went home, feeling very glad to have his nails growing again. It was wonderful to see them grow! In a week's time they were almost at the tips of his fingers! Billy was pleased.

And then, in school one morning, Billy quite forgot and began to nibble the nail on the first finger of his right hand! And what do you suppose happened?

The nail squealed out. Yes, it did really. '*Eeeeee!*' it squealed. '*EEEeeeee!*'

Billy was startled. His teacher looked up. 'How dare you make that noise, Billy!' she said. 'Go into the corner!'

'It was my nail that squealed,' said Billy.

'Don't tell me such silly stories,' said his teacher. And Billy had to go into the corner.

The next time that Billy bit his nails he was in church on Sunday. Oh, dear, oh, dear! He bit the nail on the little finger of his left hand – and it squealed out loudly.

'*Eeeeee! Ooooo! Eeeee!*'

Billy's father was so angry. He took Billy by the arm and marched him straight out of church. Billy didn't dare to tell his father that it was his nail that had squealed, because he felt sure his father wouldn't believe him. He was in disgrace all that day.

The next time that Billy bit his nails he was at a party. It was a most exciting one and Billy began to bite his nails.

'*Eeeeee!*' said one nail.

'*Oooooo!*' said another.

'*Ow-ow-iw-ow!*' said a third.

Everyone looked at Billy.

'Poor little boy. He doesn't feel well,' said the lady who was giving the party. She took Billy's arm and went out of the room with him. 'You had better go home, Billy,' she said. 'You are not well.'

'It was my nails that squealed like that, not me,' said poor Billy.

'Oh, no, dear,' said the lady. 'You mustn't tell silly stories like that. Here's your coat. Run home and tell your mother you don't feel well.'

Billy went home – and on the way he made up his mind that never, never again would he bite his nails.

It was simply dreadful to have them squealing like that! He would let them grow properly, and perhaps in time they would be like everyone else's nails.

So he hasn't bitten them again. He showed them to me yesterday. They are so nice and round and long – but I do wonder what will happen when he cuts them? Perhaps they won't mind that – perhaps it is only biting they don't like! What do *you* think?

The Forgotten Canary

The Forgotten Canary

THERE WAS once a little canary called Feathers. He lived in a blue cage in Katie's nursery, and he belonged to Katie.

At first Katie loved Feathers and looked after him well. Each day she cleaned his cage, gave him new seed and fresh water. At teatime she gave him a lump of sugar, and every day she looked for a bit of groundsel to give him for a treat.

Then, when it was no longer fun to look after him, Katie began to get tired of him. She gave him no groundsel. She forgot his lump of sugar.

One day she didn't clean his cage. Another day she

didn't give him any fresh seed, because she thought he had enough. She didn't guess how he looked forward to turning over fresh seed every morning.

And then, worst of all, she forgot his water. Mother saw that he had very little water and scolded Katie, and the little girl was ashamed. For four days she cleaned his cage properly, gave him food and water, and even picked a bit of groundsel for him and put in a dish of water for a bath.

Then she forgot again. Feathers was very unhappy. He could not sing because he was so thirsty. Twenty times a day he went to his water dish and looked at it with his head on one side, hoping and hoping that there might be just a drop of water there – but of course there wasn't.

'Tweet, tweet!' called Feathers loudly. Katie was putting her dolls to bed and took no notice. 'TWEET, TWEET!' called Feathers again. It wasn't a bit of good.

I'm in this little cage and I can't get out to find food

and water for myself, thought the canary sadly. *If I were a sparrow I could hunt for seed for myself. If I were a chaffinch I could go to the nearest pool for a drink. But I'm a canary in a cage, and I can't look after myself at all.*

Poor little canary! He had no drink for two days, and the seed in his little dish was nothing but husks. It was dreadful! He drooped his little yellow head and thought he would die.

'Have you fed the canary this morning?' said Mother, putting her head in at the door.

Katie knew she hadn't – and she knew that Mother would be very angry with her if she found out that her canary had no food. So what did the naughty little girl say, 'Oh, yes, Mother, Feathers is quite all right!'

It was a naughty story, and Katie was ashamed of herself for telling it, and went very red. But Mother didn't see her red face. She was busy and went off to do some ironing.

'I can give Feathers some food and water at once,' Katie said to herself. 'Then it won't be a story.'

But it *was* a story, wasn't it? And do you know, just as Katie was going to take down the cage to clean it, Mother called her, 'Katie! I want you to go and get some cakes for me. Hurry now, because there isn't much time.'

I'll do the canary afterwards, thought Katie, and ran off. She didn't remember to do the canary when she came back, though Feathers was hoping and hoping that she would.

The next morning, very early, a little brown sparrow looked in at the nursery window. He sometimes came to have a word with Feathers. He chirruped to him, 'Chirrup! Chirrup! How are you, Feathers?'

'Not at all well,' said poor Feathers sadly. 'I've had no food and no water for a long time. I think I shall soon die.'

'I'll bring you something to eat,' said the sparrow. He flew off and came back with a few seeds in his beak. He sat on the cage wire and dropped them through to Feathers.

'I can't bring you water,' he said. 'I don't know how to. But, Feathers, I'm going to tell the little pixie who lives in the rockery. She may be able to help you.'

So he flew off to tell Binks the pixie. Binks was angry, and sorry to hear about poor Feathers.

'I won't let that horrid Katie have a canary!' she said. 'I won't, I won't! I'll rescue Feathers myself and set him free.'

'But, Binks, if you do that, everyone will see him flying about, and he'll be caught again,' said the sparrow. 'You know what a bright yellow he is. If only he were a common brown like us, he'd never be noticed.'

'Don't bother me for a moment,' said Binks. 'I want to think.' So she thought hard, while the sparrow sat by in silence.

'I believe there is a pot of brown paint in the gardener's shed,' said Binks at last, getting up. 'I'll rescue Feathers, paint him brown and let him live with you sparrows. You can teach him how to find seeds, can't you?'

'Certainly,' said the sparrow, pleased. 'May I come with you and see what you do, Binks?'

He went with Binks. The pixie flew in at the nursery window. Katie was having her breakfast downstairs with her mother. There was no one in the nursery.

Binks set down the brown paint on the windowsill and flew to the cage. 'Feathers! Are you well enough to fly out of the window if I open your cage door and set you free?' she asked.

'I think so,' said the poor canary, who felt very weak indeed. 'I'll try. But what will Katie say when she finds my cage empty? Hadn't we better leave a note for her to say that I've gone?'

'Yes,' said Binks. 'We *will* leave a note – and I will write it!'

She went to where Katie kept her writing things

and tore off a sheet of paper. She took a pencil and wrote. This is what Binks said:

Dear Katie,

I have gone away because you don't give me food or water and I am nearly dead. You are a horrid, unkind girl.

Tweets from Feathers.

Binks opened the door of the cage and Feathers flew out. He managed to get to the windowsill, and there he perched, feeling rather wobbly. Binks put the note at the bottom of the cage, and then shut the cage door again. She flew to the windowsill and picked up the pot of paint.

'Just come with me to the holly tree,' she said. 'It isn't bare like the other trees, and you can hide there while I paint you brown. Then you'll be like the sparrows.'

They went to the holly tree, and in the shade of its

prickly leaves Binks painted Feathers a plain brown colour. She even painted a little black bib under his chin, just like the father sparrows were wearing then, and little bars of white in his wing feathers.

When he was finished he sat in the sun to dry. He looked like a sparrow, except his legs were a pinker colour and not quite so thick as a sparrow's.

The sparrows came round him and made him welcome. 'Come and we'll show you where the best seeds are to be found,' they chirruped. 'You shall be one of us!'

So Feathers went with them, and soon became very clever at finding food and water. How lovely it was to drink from puddles, and to peck at wild bits of groundsel whenever he found them!

And what about Katie? Well, after breakfast she came into the nursery, and remembered her canary. 'Oh, dear!' she said. 'I meant to have cleaned the cage yesterday and I forgot again. What a nuisance! I really must do it today.'

So she took down the cage, but to her enormous surprise Feathers wasn't there! She looked and she looked, but Feathers simply wasn't there at all.

She ran to the door and called her mother. 'Mother! Mother! Have you let Feathers out?'

'Of course not,' said Mother, running up. 'He must be there! The door of the cage is shut.'

But the canary was certainly gone. Mother spied the little note in the bottom of the cage. She opened the door, put in her hand and picked up the note. She read it.

Mother put down the note and looked at Katie, who had gone very red. 'Katie! What a dreadful thing! So that's why your canary has gone. Well, it serves you right. If you can't look after something in your care, you have no right to keep it. I'm ashamed of you.'

Katie burst into tears. She remembered how sweetly Feathers had sung. She remembered how he put his little yellow head on one side when she spoke to him.

She remembered how prettily he splashed in his bath. Now he was gone and would never come back.

'It serves you right,' said Mother. 'I only hope poor little Feathers will be able to feed himself out in the garden.'

She needn't have worried. Feathers is *quite* all right with the sparrows. The only thing is – he got caught in the rain the other day, and some of the brown paint came off, showing his yellow colour underneath. So if you see a sparrow with patches of yellow, you'll know who it is – it's Feathers!

Fussy Philip

Fussy Philip

ONCE UPON a time there was a boy who made a fuss about everything. You really would have laughed if you had lived in his home to see the way he made a fuss about even the very smallest things.

The fussing began each morning when he got up. He always wanted to wear something different from what his mother said he should wear.

'Oh, dear! Must I wear that red jersey today?' he would say. 'I do hate it. It's tight at my neck.'

'But you loved wearing it yesterday!' his mother would say in surprise. 'Well, wear the blue one.'

'Oh, Mummy, that's too thick,' Philip would say.

And then he would fuss about his shoes.

'I don't want to wear my sandals. The boys laugh at them. And my lace ones have a nail inside that sticks into my foot. Oh, dear, what shall I wear?'

At mealtimes the fussing was terrible. If there were eggs, Philip would pout and say, 'I don't like eggs. I want fish.'

And if there was fish he would poke at it with his fork and fuss about bones. 'I am sure there are bones in my fish cake, I'm sure there are. I shall get one in my throat and it will choke me.'

'Don't be silly, Philip,' his mother would say patiently. 'There aren't bones in fish cakes.'

'Well, I had a bone in one last week,' Philip would grumble. 'Can't I have an egg?'

Everyone at school called him Fussy Philip. He fussed about his books. He fussed about his pencils. He fussed because someone else hung their coat on his peg by mistake.

One day he fussed so much that his teacher got

really angry with him. She had told the class to rule some straight lines in their geography books, so Philip had opened his desk to get out his book.

'Oh my, where's it gone?' he fussed. 'I know I put it here with my history book. Miss Brown, did I give my book to you yesterday? I can't find it.'

'Don't make such a fuss,' said Miss Brown. 'I expect it's somewhere in your desk. Look carefully and don't chatter so much.'

Well, of course, the book was there, next to the history book after all. But then Philip couldn't find his ruler. He began to fuss all over again.

'Who's taken my ruler? Has anyone borrowed my ruler? Oh, bother, bother, now my ruler's gone! Miss Brown, I've got my geography book but I haven't got my ruler.'

'Be quiet, Philip,' said Miss Brown, who was getting very tired of him. 'Borrow John's. He's finished ruling his lines.'

'But, Miss Brown, what can have happened to my

ruler?' fussed Philip. 'Honestly, it was here this morning. I don't want to borrow John's. It's a bit broken at the edge and it doesn't make nice lines. I want my own ruler.'

'Philip, if you don't borrow someone else's and get on, the lesson will be over before you've even begun it!' said Miss Brown. 'Look – isn't that your ruler on the top of your desk?'

'Oh, good gracious me, yes, it is!' Philip said. 'Of course, I remember now. I got it out first and put it there. And all this time I've been hunting in my desk. How funny!'

'It's not a bit funny,' said Miss Brown crossly. 'It's just silly. Do stop fussing and get on.'

John, who sat next to Philip, took up his pen and shook it. It was a fine new fountain pen, just filled with ink. A drop flew from the nib and landed on Philip's jersey sleeve. How he fussed again!

'Miss Brown! Oh, Miss Brown, do look what John has done! He's shaken a blob of ink on to my jersey sleeve. Oh, Miss Brown, my mother will be cross, won't she?'

'PHILIP! Be quiet,' said Miss Brown in quite a fierce tone. 'Your jersey is dark blue and the ink is dark blue and the blob won't show at all when it's dry. Press a bit of blotting paper on it.'

'Miss Brown, now my blotting paper is gone!' said Philip, rummaging through his desk in a hurry. 'Oh, goodness, who's borrowed that now? It was such a nice new piece. My mother gave it to me yesterday. Miss Brown, may I have a new piece out of the cupboard, please?'

'Philip, I'm tired of you,' said Miss Brown suddenly. 'I never met such a fusser in all my life. If you say one word more about anything in this class, you can just put on your coat and cap and go home. You hold up the whole class with your silly fussing.'

Well, Philip got rather a shock when Miss Brown said that. He didn't say one word more but got on with his work. But the fussing began all over again when playtime came after the lesson was finished.

'Line up,' said Miss Brown, when the bell rang for playtime. 'That's right. Now – right turn – march out! Come in as soon as the bell rings – and no dawdling, please!'

'Miss Brown, have we to put our coats on, as it's a bit cold?' asked Philip. 'You see, Miss Brown, I'm only just over a cold and my mother—'

'Put on your coat, cap, scarf, gloves and boots if you want to, Philip, but DON'T FUSS!' said Miss Brown.

'Oh, but, Miss Brown, I didn't come in boots,' said Philip. 'Do you think I ought to have? Nobody else did.'

The other children marched out and soon ran into the garden to play. Only Philip was left.

'Philip, I'm so tired of you that I simply wouldn't care if you went out to play in your bare feet,' said Miss Brown. 'I don't even care whether you go out to play at all. In another second I shall probably tell you to sit in the corner over there and think for fifteen minutes about fussing and how silly it is.'

'Oh, Miss Brown, don't do that,' said Philip in alarm, and he tried to go out of the schoolroom in such a hurry that he fell over a little table and knocked down the pile of papers there.

My goodness me! How he fussed over that! 'Oh, dear, oh, dear! Those are the papers I arranged for the painting lesson. Look, Miss Brown, they're all upset, and I did pile them together so neatly. This one's got dirty. Shall I get another sheet out of the cupboard?'

'Philip, you can stay and fuss all by yourself,' said Miss Brown. 'I'm going into the garden. Goodbye.'

She walked out. Philip fussed over the sheets of paper and arranged them all beautifully again. Then he went to the cupboard to get a sheet instead of the one that had got dirty. He couldn't find one that was exactly the same size as the others.

Oh, dear, now that means somebody will have a different

sheet, he thought, and he looked all over the shelf to find what he wanted.

Well, by the time the bell rang for the children to come in from their play, Philip had just finished arranging the painting papers again. How upset he was when he found that he had missed the whole of playtime! He went to Miss Brown.

'Miss Brown! It's not fair! I've not had any playtime at all. I'm awfully unlucky this morning, really I am.'

'Well, you're going to be lucky now,' said Miss Brown in despair. 'I can't put up with you any more today. Go into the playground and play there by yourself. You fuss so much that you don't get a single thing done, so you might as well go out and be by yourself. At least the rest of the class will be able to get something done! I don't wonder the others call you Fussy Philip! Go along out, Fussy Philip – and don't come back till you feel better!'

Philip was very hurt and upset at being called Fussy Philip. He began to cry, but Miss Brown wasn't going to have that. She took him firmly by the shoulders and put him out of the schoolroom. She shut the door.

Everybody was pleased. It was so disturbing to have someone fussing around the whole time. Philip stood outside the door, crying. He wondered what to do. He didn't dare to go back into the room again. Miss Brown really was in a temper.

He went to the cloakroom and put on his coat and cap. Then he went out into the school garden. He wandered up to the very end of it, where it was rather wild and overgrown. He sat down on a barrow there and cried tears all down his face. He felt terribly sorry for himself.

'Hallo!' said a voice in surprise. 'What's the matter? Don't cry! I can't bear to see people cry!'

Philip looked up in surprise. He saw a tiny little old woman, not even as tall as himself. She had the green eyes of the little folk, so Philip knew at once she belonged to the fairies. He dried his eyes.

'Old woman, I'm very unhappy. My teacher is angry with me and she's turned me out of the schoolroom. I'm missing storytime, which is the nicest time of all the week. Now I'm here all by myself, sitting on this barrow, very lonely and sad.'

'Poor lamb!' said the little old woman, and she took his hand in hers. 'Come with me. I'll give you a few treats! I'm just on my way to catch the bus to go to the Silver Pixie's party. You come too! You'd love that.'

'Ooh!' said Philip, his eyes shining and his heart jumping for joy. 'That would be marvellous. I'll come with you now.'

'Well, we've got to hurry,' said the old woman. 'The bus is due at the old oak tree in about two minutes. Come along.'

Off they went, through a small gap in the hedge. Philip felt very pleased. 'Ha! Miss Brown has been horrid to me – but I'm going to have a good time. Won't she be surprised when I go back and tell her!'

Philip and the little old woman hurried across the field to the old oak tree. But on the way Philip got a tiny little stone in his shoe. It really wasn't much bigger than a grain of sand, but you know what a fusser Philip was! 'Oh! I've got a stone in my shoe!' he said, and he began to limp as if he had a stone as big as an egg there! The old woman stopped at once.

'Dear, dear! Let's get it out!' she said. 'But, oh – I wonder if we'd better not stop. We may miss the bus.'

'It does hurt me dreadfully,' fussed Philip, limping badly. 'Oh, dear me, what an unlucky boy I am!'

'I can't bear to see you limping like that,' said the old woman. 'Sit down on the bank and I'll get the stone out for you.'

Philip simply loved being fussed over. So down he sat and let the old woman take off his shoe. She shook out the tiny little stone, and was just going to put his shoe on again when there came a rumbling noise.

'It's the bus!' cried the old woman. 'Quick, run!'

Philip jumped up and ran – with only one shoe

on! He trod on a thorn and yelled! He trod on a big stone and yelled again.

'Come on, come on!' said the old woman, and pulled him across the field to the bus.

But, alas, they missed it! The bus conductor – who, most surprisingly, was a large brown rabbit – didn't see them, and the bus rumbled away without them.

'Oh, bother!' said the old woman. 'It's gone. What a pity you fussed about that tiny stone! It really couldn't have hurt you. Now we'll have to walk to the Silver Pixie's, and we shall be late.'

'How can I walk with only one shoe on?' said Philip crossly. 'Have you got my left shoe?'

'No,' said the old woman. 'Didn't you bring it with you, you silly boy?'

'No,' said Philip. 'We'd better go back for it.' So back they went to look for it, but they couldn't find it anywhere.

'Well, you'll have to walk in one shoe if you want to go to the party,' said the old woman. 'Come on.'

'I do wish I hadn't missed the treat of going in that funny bus,' said Philip, limping along. 'It had a rabbit for a conductor.'

'The driver is a weasel,' said the old woman. 'The tickets are biscuits. You eat them instead of throwing them away.'

'Gracious!' said Philip. 'What a very good idea! I wish they'd do that on our buses!'

They walked on for a good way, and at last came to an enormous tree.

'The Silver Pixie lives at the top,' said the old woman. 'It's too tiring to climb up. We'll fly.'

She undid her shawl and shook out two beautiful wings that had been folded neatly underneath, rather like two fans. Philip stared at them in surprise.

'Ooh! What gorgeous wings!' he said. 'I haven't got any. I can't fly up the tree.'

'I'll get you some,' said the old woman, and she rapped on the trunk of the tree. A little door flew open and an old brownie peered out.

'What do you want?' he asked.

'Will you lend this boy a pair of wings, Longbeard?' asked the old woman. 'We want to fly up the tree.'

'Come in,' said the brownie, and the two went into his round treehouse. Philip couldn't help feeling excited. The brownie put a box on his table and opened it. It was full of wings of all kinds.

'I should think these would fit you,' said the brownie, and he took out a pair of bright red ones. He began to fasten them on Philip's shoulders.

'They do feel funny,' said Philip, beginning to fuss as usual. 'They feel sort of tight.'

'Well, you surely don't want them to be loose, do you?' asked the brownie. 'It's not much good flying with loose wings, I can tell you! Well – try these.'

He took out a pair of green ones. But Philip didn't like them very much. 'I don't like green,' he said. 'It's unlucky.'

'Green is not unlucky!' said the brownie crossly. 'Who told you that silly tale? Are the trees unlucky?

Are the bushes unlucky? Is the grass unlucky? No, they are all beautiful and happy. What a fussy boy you are! Look – here is a dear little pair of blue wings with silver edges.'

They were very pretty wings, but rather small. 'I don't believe they would carry me up high,' said Philip. 'I'd be afraid of falling down if I wore those wings.'

The brownie lost his temper. He slammed down the lid of his box and threw it into a corner. 'Oh, there's no pleasing you!' he said. 'I'm not lending any of my beautiful wings to a fusspot like you!'

'I'm not a fusspot!' said Philip, who didn't like that name at all. But he wasn't allowed to say a word more, because the brownie pushed him out of the tree and shut his door with a bang. The old woman looked at Philip sadly.

'You'll have to climb the tree now, instead of flying up,' she said. 'I'm beginning to think you're rather silly. Well, I'm off into the air. I'll see you at the top of the tree.'

She flew up like an enormous butterfly. Philip began to climb the tree, wishing and wishing that he had taken the first pair of wings he had been offered.

It took him a long time to climb to the top. When he got there he was tired out. He sat down to rest on a big branch. He heard the sounds of laughter and chattering nearby, and saw that just above him, on a broad, flat cloud that rested on the topmost branches, the party was going on. As he looked up, the old woman peeped over and saw him.

'Come along,' she said. 'I hope you're not too tired.'

Philip climbed up to the cloud. 'I'm dreadfully tired!' he said. 'My poor arms! How they ache with trying to pull myself up higher and higher. And my left foot is sore because I haven't its shoe.'

'Well, never mind, we won't let you dance or play around,' said the old woman.

'Oh, but I'd like to,' said Philip, looking joyfully at all the little folk having a merry time on the flat, soft cloud.

'No, no,' said the old woman. 'It would be bad for you. Look – here is the Silver Pixie. Say how-do-you-do to him!'

The Silver Pixie was a tall and beautiful creature dressed in shining silver. He even had silver hair and teeth, and he was the grandest person that Philip had ever seen.

'You must have something to eat,' he said. 'Hi, servants! Bring jellies here!'

Two small elves brought a big dish on which trembled a large yellow jelly. It looked marvellous.

'I like pink jelly the best, really,' said Philip, taking the spoon and plate offered him by the Silver Pixie. 'But this looks lovely.'

'Fancy fussing about whether the jelly is yellow or pink!' whispered an elf.

The Silver Pixie turned and spoke to them. 'Take this yellow jelly away and see if you can find a pink one.'

The elves carried away the big dish. They didn't

come back for a long time. When they arrived again, they were empty-handed. 'The pink jelly is all eaten,' they said to the pixie.

'Oh, well, never mind, I'll have the yellow jelly,' said Philip, who by now was wishing that he hadn't said anything about the colour. But alas! When the yellow jelly dish was found, it was empty! The guests had eaten it all!

'I'm afraid you won't be able to have any jelly,' said the Silver Pixie. 'I'm really very sorry. I'll have some ices sent to you.'

But before the ices could arrive a tall brownie got up and clapped his hands. 'Speeches!' he said. 'Be quiet, everyone, while I make a speech to thank the Silver Pixie for his marvellous party!'

Poor Philip! Everyone sat still, even the servants, so no one brought him any ices or any other food either. He was very sad. He saw the old woman nearby and thought he would ask her to get him a biscuit. So he crept over the cloud to where she sat listening to the brownie's speech. But suddenly Philip reached a thin place in the cloud – and he fell through it!

Down he went, and down and down! He fell through the tree branches, bump – bump – bump! What a dreadfully tall tree! And then bump! He was on the ground. The door in the trunk flew open and the old brownie looked out at him.

'Gracious! I wondered whatever it was coming down the tree like that!' he said. 'Is that the way you usually come down trees?'

'No,' sobbed Philip, feeling his bumps and bruises. 'Oh, what an unlucky fellow I am! I've missed every single treat I might have had! I didn't ride in that funny bus. I didn't get a pair of wings from you. I didn't get any jelly to eat at the party. And now I've fallen down the tree from top to bottom.'

'If you take my advice – which you won't – I could cure you of your bad luck!' said the brownie. 'I know what's the matter with you, my lad – it's fussing. Didn't you know that people who fuss always miss the best things in life? Ah, you'll miss all the treats while you're a boy – and when you grow up into a fusser nothing will ever go right for you. You're a fussy, fussy fusser!'

Philip tried to catch the old brownie but he ran into his house and shut the door. The boy limped back to school, crying. All the children had gone home and the school was shut. Philip sat down on the step and thought hard.

'It was all because of my stupid fussing that things went wrong,' he said to himself. 'But how can I stop? Oh, I wish I could!'

Well, I expect he will try, but it's very hard to stop once you've really begun. So, for goodness' sake, don't you be a Fussy Philip, will you? I wouldn't like you to miss all the good things going – you're much too nice!

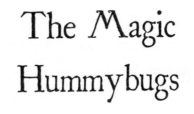

The Magic
Hummybugs

The Magic Hummybugs

THERE WERE once two naughty little children called Thomas and Polly. They were both greedy, and if they could possibly take a cake from the cake tin, a biscuit from the biscuit jar or a sweet when nobody was looking, they did.

So you see they were not at all honest. Sometimes they were caught and well scolded, and sometimes they were not caught. Their mother was unhappy about them, but she couldn't seem to make them any better.

But one day they took sweets belonging to old Dame Quick-Eyes – ah, that was a silly thing to do!

I'll tell you all about it.

Dame Quick-Eyes lived in a little cottage all by herself. She sometimes did people's washing, and she sometimes did people's mending. Polly often took her a basket of socks and stockings to darn, and the old dame was glad of the work to do. She had such good eyes that she could see perfectly well without spectacles.

Now one morning, on their way to school, Thomas and Polly had to leave some pillowcases for Dame Quick-Eyes to wash. They knocked at her door but nobody answered.

'She's out!' said Polly. 'Shall we leave the parcel on her doorstep?'

'No, we'll put it in at the kitchen window,' said Thomas. 'It's usually open.'

So they went round to the back and, sure enough, the kitchen window was open. Polly pushed the parcel on to the table there – and then she caught sight of something.

It was a bag of humbugs! Do you know what humbugs are like? They are those lovely big, striped peppermint sweets that last such a long time! Well, Dame Quick-Eyes was very fond of humbugs, and always had a bag of them by her side when she did her mending. And there was the bag she had bought the day before, lying on the table.

'Ooh!' said Polly and Thomas at the same moment, staring at the lovely bag of humbugs.

'Let's take one each,' said Thomas. 'She won't know.'

So those bad children took one big humbug each, out of Dame Quick-Eyes' bag. They were big black and white striped sweets, and the children knew they would not have time to suck them before they got to school. So Thomas tore two pages out of a notebook he carried, and wrapped one humbug up for himself and one for Polly. Polly put hers in her pocket and Thomas put away his. They meant to suck them at playtime.

Off they went to school. They took off their hats

and coats and went to take their places. Thomas sat in the middle of the class, and Polly sat at the back.

Now, although the children didn't know it, those humbugs had been bought at a little pixie sweet shop in the middle of Ho-Ho Wood. Dame Quick-Eyes sometimes did washing for the pixies there, and she always bought her sweets at this shop because they were so delicious.

Now those pixie humbugs had a little magic in them that made them hum whenever they got warm. You may have wondered why they should be called *hum*bugs – well, of course, it is because any bit of magic in them makes them *hum* loudly as soon as they get warm. In Fairyland they are called hummybugs, but we just call them humbugs for short.

Well, it wasn't long before the humbugs in the two children's pockets began to get warm. So, of course, they started to hum!

'Zzzzzzzzzz!' went the humbug in Thomas's pocket and 'Zzzzzzzzzz!' went the one in Polly's. The two children opened their eyes wide in surprise when they heard this noise. It sounded like a bumblebee buzzing. Polly and Thomas looked around their desks to see if a bee was there.

'Zzzzzzzz-zzzz!' said Thomas's humbug loudly.

'Zzzzzzzzzz!' said Polly's humbug too.

'Who is making that noise?' said the teacher angrily.

Nobody said a word, except the two humbugs. And they answered cheerfully and loudly, 'Zzzzzzzzzz! Zzzzzzzz!'

'Somebody is humming!' said the teacher.

Somebody – or something – certainly was!

'Zzzzzzzzzzzzz!' Everyone stared at Thomas and Polly, for there was no doubt the noise came from them.

'Thomas! Polly! Stop making that noise at once!' said the teacher.

'Please, we're not making any noise,' said Thomas.

'Zzzzzzzzzzz!' said the humbugs, both at once.

'You naughty, disobedient children!' said the

teacher angrily. 'Be quiet at once!'

'Zzzzzzzzzzz!' said the humbugs, quite enjoying themselves.

'Come out here,' said the teacher sternly. Polly and Thomas walked out and stood in the front of the class.

'Now you'll just stay standing out there till you can behave yourselves,' said the teacher. 'If you hum any more I shall keep you in at playtime.'

'Zzzzzzzzzzzzzzzzzzzzzzzzz!' went the humbugs, as loudly as ever they could.

The teacher stared at the two red-faced children in surprise. She couldn't think how they dared to disobey like that.

'Is it something you have got in your pockets that is making this noise?' she said suddenly. 'Turn out everything you have there, please.'

The two children turned out their pockets. Thomas put out a handkerchief, a pocketknife, a piece of rubber, two bits of string, one marble, a notebook and the humbug wrapped up in paper. Polly put out a handkerchief, a brown ha'penny, a doll's bonnet and the humbug wrapped in paper.

Well, as soon as the humbugs found themselves out in the cold air, they stopped humming and were perfectly quiet.

The teacher looked carefully at everything. 'Put them back,' she said. 'I can see nothing there that would make a noise. I see you have both stopped humming now. Go back to your seats and don't let me hear another word from you for the rest of the morning.'

The children went back to their seats. They couldn't understand it. Whatever was making that noise? If they had found bees in their pockets they wouldn't have been at all surprised. But there were no bees there at all.

They began to do their writing. The humbugs got warm again. They began to hum, quite quietly at first, but more loudly as they got nice and warm.

'Zzzzzzzzzz!' said the one in Thomas's pocket.

'Zzzzzzzzzzzzz!' sang Polly's humbug gaily.

Everyone looked up. The teacher frowned and rapped on the desk. 'Polly! Thomas! You have begun to hum again. You will lose your playtime.'

'Zzzzz-zzz-zzz-zz!' hummed the two humbugs, sounding quite pleased. 'Zzz-zzz-zzz-zzz!'

'Go out of the room,' said the teacher. 'I won't have you in here, disturbing the class.'

Thomas and Polly went out of the room and stood behind the door. How they hoped that the headmaster wouldn't come along and see them there!

Well, he did! He came walking along, and when he saw the two children standing outside the door with drooping heads he stopped in surprise.

'And what are you standing out here for, instead of working in the classroom?' he asked sternly.

Thomas and Polly opened their mouths to answer, but the humbugs got in first. 'ZZZZZZZZZZZ!' they hummed, and the headmaster stared in the greatest astonishment.

'You had better come to my study,' he said. The

two children followed him, wondering what was going to happen.

'I believe it's those humbugs we took from Dame Quick-Eyes,' whispered Thomas to Polly. 'I believe they are humming. There must be some magic in them. We'd better throw them away when we get the chance.'

But they didn't have a chance, for they were soon in the headmaster's study. He sat down and looked at the two children sternly.

'Now what is the meaning of this?' he asked.

'Zzz-zzz-zzz-zzz!' went the humbugs gaily. The headmaster could hardly believe his ears. He was just about to speak very sharply indeed to the children, when someone went by the open window, carrying a basket of washing. It was Dame Quick-Eyes, taking back the headmaster's clean shirts.

Now Dame Quick-Eyes had quick ears as well as eyes, and as soon as she heard that humming sound she knew quite well what it was. She peeped in at the window.

'Zzzzzzzzzzzzzzzzzzzzzzzz!' went the humbugs cheerfully. Dame Quick-Eyes grinned. She guessed at once that the two children had been to her house and taken her humbugs. When the sweets had begun to hum, the children had got into trouble. Served them right!

Dame Quick-Eyes called in through the window. 'Good morning, Mr Headmaster. I think I can tell you what is making that noise. Look in the children's pockets and you will find some of my hummybugs. It is they that are making that noise!'

It wasn't long before the humbugs were on the headmaster's desk – but, of course, they stopped humming as soon as they were out of the warm pockets.

'Pick one up in your hand and warm it, sir,' said Dame Quick-Eyes. The headmaster did so – and at once the humbug, feeling the warmth there, began to hum cheerfully.

'Zzzzzzzzzzz!' it sang. 'Zzzzzzzzz!'

'Good gracious me!' said the headmaster, in the greatest surprise. 'Where did these come from?'

The children went very red. Polly began to cry. 'We t-t-t-took them out of a b-b-b-bag we saw on Dame Quick-Eyes' t-t-t-table this morning!' she sobbed.

'That is stealing,' said the headmaster sternly. 'I've a good mind to make you keep these humbugs in your pockets for a week or two, so that they may tell everyone of your naughty ways.'

'Please don't!' begged Thomas and Polly. 'We'll never, never do such a thing again!'

They didn't. They threw the humbugs away on a rubbish heap, and there they will stay till someone lights a bonfire, and then what a surprise the gardener will get! You know what he'll hear, don't you, as soon as those humbugs get warm. 'Zzzzzzzz! Zzzzzzz! Zzzzzzzzzzz!'

A Little Thing that
Made a Big Thing

A Little Thing that
Made a Big Thing

JOHN HAD a ball. It was a fine ball, because it could bounce higher than John himself, and it was bright red and green. Wherever John went, that ball went too.

'I don't think you had better take the ball out into the street with you,' his mother said. 'I don't like to see children playing ball in the street. Sooner or later the ball always goes into the road, and that makes motorists very nervous indeed.'

'All right, Mother,' said John. But he didn't do what he was told. Instead of leaving the ball at home, he put it into his pocket when he went to tea with his Auntie Sue. He was late when he went, so he ran all the way, and didn't play with his ball. But he had plenty of time when he was on his way back. He took out his precious ball and bounced it.

My goodness me, how that ball did bounce! John bounced it harder than ever, just to see how high it really *would* bounce. It flew above his head, and then fell. John put out his hand to catch it.

But he missed the ball, and it fell to the ground, on to the pavement. John was at the top of the hill that led down to the town, so the ball began rolling. John sprang after it. His foot touched it and it shot out into the road.

John ran after it. Did he look and see if anything was coming? No! Children hardly ever do when they play with a ball in the street. They see the ball and nothing else! John was just like that. He darted after his ball.

There was the screech of brakes being put on hard, and everyone looked round. John was scared at the noise, remembered that he was in the road and hopped back quickly to the pavement, where he was safe. He looked to see what had made the noise.

A car had been coming along over the top of the hill at a fast speed. It had suddenly seen John rushing out and had put on its brakes very suddenly, making the screeching noise that everyone had heard.

It swung to the other side of the road to avoid John, and crashed into a barrow of apples, being wheeled by Mr Pip, the apple man. The barrow was smashed. Mr Pip jumped to safety. Hundreds of apples were spilt and went rolling down the street!

The milkman was coming up the hill, driving his horse. When the horse heard the crash of the car going into the apple barrow, it was frightened. It reared up, swung right round and galloped off at top speed down the hill!

The milkman fell out. He got up at once, and yelled after his horse, 'Hie there! Hie! Come back! Whoa, whoa!'

But the frightened horse took no notice. It galloped

down the hill, going faster and faster.

'Runaway horse, runaway horse!' shouted everyone. The milk cart bumped against the kerb, and about fifty bottles of milk jumped out, flew through the air and landed with a crash. Creamy milk began to pour down the hill in a steady stream. The grocer's cat was delighted, and went to lick up what she could.

The horse galloped on. He was on the wrong side of the road, and he knocked over a man on a bicycle. The bicycle had its front wheel badly bent, and the man could not ride it any more. But still the horse went on.

Down at the bottom of the hill was the river. A bridge went over it. The horse galloped towards the bridge, its cart swaying behind it. A car suddenly came over the bridge from the opposite side, and the driver looked in horror at the galloping horse.

What would happen? Would the horse crash into the car, and hurt itself? Would the driver be killed? No one knew. Everyone stood and watched in fear.

The driver of the car twisted the steering wheel round as sharply as he could. He could not stop his car at once because he was going too fast. The car ran over the pavement, crashed through the bridge railings and fell with a terrific splash into the river below!

'Get the driver out! He'll be drowned!' everyone cried. By now the galloping horse had been stopped by a big policeman, who tied it to a post and then ran to help the man in the car.

John had watched everything in the greatest horror. He ran down the hill after the milk cart. He saw the man being knocked off his bicycle. He saw the car swerve and fall into the river. He knew that car. Yes – John knew that car quite well!

It's my daddy's car! he thought, and he felt suddenly sick. *It's Daddy in that car! He's fallen into the river. He'll be drowned. Oh, Daddy, Daddy!*

He saw his father taken out of the sinking car. He watched him laid on the banks of the river, while men tried to bring him to life again. John cried so bitterly that he could hardly see at all.

His father opened his eyes at last. John flung himself on the wet, cold man. 'Daddy! I was afraid you'd be drowned. Oh, Daddy, it was all my fault!'

'Silly boy! It was the milk horse's fault!' said somebody.

'It wasn't, it wasn't!' sobbed John. 'It was me and my ball. My ball ran into the road. I ran after it. A car swerved away from me and ran into the apple man's barrow. The crash it made frightened the milkman's horse, and it ran away. And that galloping horse met you and made you fall into the river with your car.'

Poor John. Everything he said was true, wasn't it? His father talked to him very gravely that night.

'I must pay the apple man for his lost apples and broken barrow,' he said. 'I must pay the milkman for his spilt milk and smashed bottles. I must pay for the cyclist's wheel to be mended. I must pay a great deal of money to get my poor spoilt car out of the river. John, John, you have a very big lesson to learn. A little thing may be a very little thing – but it may cause a very much bigger thing. See what running into the road after your ball has done!'

'I wish it could be put into a story for other children,' said John, 'then they will know it too!'

So it has, and you've just read it!

Polly's P's and Q's

Polly's P's and Q's

HAVE YOU ever heard anyone say to a boy or girl, 'Now just mind your P's and Q's'?

Well, Polly was a little girl who *didn't* mind hers! She was always forgetting her pleases and thank yous. The P's are the pleases you see, and the Q's are the thank yous. If you say, 'Thank you', you will hear the Q at the end!

'Will you have some more pudding?' Polly's mother would say. And Polly would answer, 'Yes.'

'Yes, what?' her mother would say. '*How* many times must I tell you to say "Please"? It does sound so rude to say "Yes" like that. You should say,

"Yes, please, Mummy".'

Then she would give Polly her pudding, and the little girl would take it – and forget to say 'Thank you'! She really was dreadful!

One day her Aunt Jessica came to tea with Polly, Mummy and Gran. Polly was a bit afraid of her, because she was rather strict and she always said that Polly was spoilt.

Aunt Jessica brought out a packet of butterscotch. She nearly always had some sweets in her bag. She offered some to Mummy. 'Thank you, Jessica,' said Mummy, and took a piece.

'Would you like some butterscotch too, Polly?' asked Aunt Jessica.

'Yes,' said Polly at once. She loved butterscotch.

Aunt Jessica glared. 'I'll give you another chance, Polly,' she said crossly. 'Would you like to have a piece of my butterscotch?'

'Yes,' said Polly. She didn't think of saying 'Please', you see!

'No pleases today, I see,' said Aunt Jessica, putting away her packet of sweets. 'Well, no pleases, no butterscotch!'

'Please!' said Polly. Aunt Jessica looked very cross still, but she undid the packet and offered it to Polly. Polly took a piece and began to unwrap the paper.

But Aunt Jessica put out her hand and took the butterscotch from her. She wrapped it up again and put it into the packet.

'You bad-mannered little girl!' she said. 'Not even a "Thank you" now!'

'Oh, thank you!' cried Polly. But it was too late this time. Aunt Jessica put the butterscotch away in her bag. She turned to Mummy.

'Alice, I can't *think* why you don't teach Polly her manners!' she said. 'I'm really ashamed of my niece. What *must* people think of her when she goes out to tea and never says "Please" or "Thank you"?'

'I don't know,' said Mummy, looking worried.

'I do try to teach her, Jessica – I really do. But she forgets so often. I really do *not* know what to do! Could *you* tell me what to do? You're so clever with children.'

'Dear me, yes, I can tell you what to do,' said Aunt Jessica at once. 'Every time she forgets her P's and Q's pin one on to her – she won't like being hung with them, I am sure – and they will remind her of what she keeps forgetting.'

'Well, that's a good idea,' said Mummy with a laugh, and she began to cut out lots of letter P's and Q's from some white cotton stuff. When she had about thirty, she stuck a safety pin into each one.

'There!' she said. 'They're all ready! Polly, here are your P's and Q's. Every time you remember one, it shall go into the wastepaper basket. But every time you forget one, it shall come to you!'

Polly thought it was a horrid idea. She made up her mind she wouldn't have a single one of the nasty letters pinned to her. She sat looking sulky.

Aunt Jessica and Mummy went on talking about something else. Polly's gran came into the room with a rosy apple. 'Would you like an apple, Polly?' she asked.

'Yes!' shouted Polly, and she ran to take it. She didn't say 'Please', and she didn't say 'Thank you'! Aunt Jessica at once took up a large white P and a large white Q from the table.

'Come here, Polly,' she said. Polly went to her slowly. Aunt Jessica pinned the P on to the front of her jersey, and the Q on to her skirt.

'There!' she said. 'There's the "Please" you forgot and the "Thank you" you forgot. They have both come to live with you!'

Polly was ashamed, but do you know, she had got into such a bad habit of forgetting her P's and Q's that she forgot them three more times before Aunt Jessica went home! So she had three more P's and three more Q's pinned on to her, back and front, before bedtime came.

'Can I take them off now?' asked Polly, when she undressed.

'Oh, no,' said Gran. 'Mummy says you must keep them on till you remember. It will be strange for you to put on your jersey and skirt tomorrow, with all these funny white letters on. I do think you are silly not to remember your P's and Q's. Other children do.'

Well, Polly didn't at all like putting on her skirt and jersey next morning, with so many white letters pinned there. She was glad that Daddy had gone to town before he saw her. He *would* have laughed at her!

At breakfast time Mummy said to Polly, 'Would you like sugar or treacle with your porridge this morning, Polly?'

'Treacle,' said Polly – and then she suddenly remembered! 'Treacle, PLEASE, Mummy!' she said.

'Good girl,' said Mummy. 'I will unpin one of the P's. Come here.' So one of the horrid P's was taken away and thrown into the wastepaper basket.

Polly was glad. *Oh, I'll soon get rid of them all!* she thought.

But it wasn't so easy. She twice forgot to say 'Please' to Gran, and three times forgot a 'Thank you'. So Gran had to pin five more letters on her. And Mummy pinned seven more by the end of the morning. Wasn't it dreadful!

'Well, this just shows you what bad manners you have, Polly,' said Mummy sadly. 'I can hardly believe you forget so often!'

That afternoon Alan came to ask if Polly could go home to tea with him. 'Can I, Mummy, PLEASE?' asked Polly.

Mummy unpinned a P and threw it away. 'Yes, you may go,' she said. 'But dear me, *I* shouldn't like to go all pinned up with P's and Q's!'

'Oh!' cried Polly in dismay. 'Must I take them with me?'

'Certainly,' said Mummy. 'You've got to get rid of them by remembering them.'

'Then I shan't go out to tea,' said Polly, and she began to cry because Alan was laughing at her skirt, all pinned over with white letters.

So she didn't go out to tea, and she was very sad indeed. She sat in a corner and cried. Gran was sorry for her.

'Cheer up, Polly,' she said. 'You know quite well that you can get rid of *all* those letters if you really try. You only need to think hard when you answer anybody. Cheer up, do! Shall I read to you for a while?'

'Yes, Gran, PLEASE!' said Polly at once. Gran unpinned a P. She took down a book and Polly got on her knee.

'Thank you, Gran!' said Polly. Off came another Q! Good!

When Gran had finished the story, Polly spoke to her. 'PLEASE, Gran, will you read another?'

Off came another P. This was fine. When the story was finished, Polly said, 'Thank you, Gran, I loved that.'

Off went a Q. Gran was surprised and glad. 'Well, you really do sound perfectly sweet when you speak like that,' she told Polly. 'Good-mannered children are always nice to be with, and it's a pleasure to hear you talk so politely.'

You will hardly believe it, but before that day was done, Polly had had every single P and Q unpinned from her skirt! Not one was left. They were all in the wastepaper basket!

'I wonder if I ought to cut some more for tomorrow!' said Mummy. 'I'd better, I think.'

'No, Mummy, THANK YOU!' said Polly at once. 'I'm always going to remember now.'

'Well, I hope you do,' said Mummy, 'because Aunt Jessica is coming again tomorrow.'

She came as usual, and this time she had a box of chocolates. She offered one to Polly.

'Thank you, Aunt Jessica,' said Polly. Aunt Jessica looked surprised, but she didn't say anything. She talked to Mummy for a bit, then she turned to Polly.

'Would you like to show me your garden?' she asked.

'Yes, please, Aunt Jessica,' said Polly, jumping up, pleased to show her pretty garden.

'Bless us all!' said Aunt Jessica, staring in astonishment at Polly. 'How did she learn such nice manners all of a sudden? Don't tell me it was the P's and Q's!'

'It was, Jessica,' said Mummy, laughing. 'You should have seen Polly yesterday morning – covered with P's and Q's from head to foot. She *did* look silly. But she suddenly made up her mind she couldn't bear it, and before she went to bed she had got rid of them all and had learnt the nicest way of speaking you can imagine!'

'Splendid!' said Aunt Jessica, and she gave Polly a hug. 'You're a nice little girl, my dear, but even the nicest people can be spoilt if they have bad manners. I shall be proud of you now, I'm sure!'

She is, because Polly didn't once have another P

or Q pinned to her. Everyone likes to have her to tea because she has such nice manners. It was a funny way of learning to mind her P's and Q's, wasn't it? I do hope you'll never have to learn in Polly's way – but I'm sure you won't!

The Dirty Little Boy

The Dirty Little Boy

THERE WAS once a boy called Tom, who seemed always to be dirty. It really didn't matter at all what he was doing – maybe only reading quietly in a chair – but when he got up he was sure to have dirty hands, knees and face and probably a hole in his shirt.

'I can't help it, Mummy!' he would say. 'I don't mean to – the dirt just comes!'

Now there came a day when the school children had been promised a great treat. There was a wonderful circus in the town, and the headmaster had said that he would take the whole school that afternoon.

'You will be here punctually at two o'clock,' he

said to the listening boys and girls. 'And you will come with clean hands, faces and knees and your best clothes on. There will be a great many people at the circus, and I want them to look at you and say, "What clean, well-behaved children!" and not, "What a set of ragamuffins!" Anyone who arrives dirty will be left behind.'

The children ran home joyfully. No school that afternoon – but a circus instead! What a treat!

Tom ran home too and told his mother.

'My goodness,' she said, 'you will really have to be clean for once, Tom! Hurry up with your lunch. I think I'll give you a good scrub, and then you can put on your best clothes.'

So Tom hurried up, and very soon he was standing in the bathroom and his mother was scrubbing his knees and hands and washing his face and ears.

'Now give your teeth a clean, Tom,' she said. 'You might as well do that too.'

At twenty minutes to two you should have seen

Tom! He shone with soap and water! His teeth gleamed. His collar was as white as snow. His clothes were clean and quite perfect – he really was a fine sight to look at, for even his hair, which would usually stick straight up, was lying smooth and shining, flat on his round head.

'Well, you look nicer than I have ever seen you look before,' said his mother, giving him a kiss. 'Now off you go – and if you get to school as clean as that, you'll do!'

'Mummy, I promise you I'll do my best,' Tom said earnestly. 'I like being clean, really I do. I don't know how it is I seem to get dirty. I will really be a good boy and go straight to school this very minute.'

Off he went, walking carefully in the very middle of the pavement and going round every puddle instead of through it as he usually did. And he was very nearly at school when he heard something that puzzled him.

There was a shed nearby that led into a big dairy – and from this shed, or rather from underneath the shed, came a pitiful whining. Tom couldn't make it out. He looked into the shed – no one was there at all, certainly no dog. Then the whining came again, and Tom looked down at the floor for it seemed that the noise came from there.

And then he saw that a drainpipe came out of the shed from beneath the floor. It ran from the dairy, under the floor of the shed and out into the road. The dog must be in there! It had got in – and it couldn't get out!

'Whatever shall I do?' wondered Tom. 'All right, all right, good dog! I'm here! I've heard you! Good dog! Don't be frightened!'

Tom knelt down on the pavement and looked down the pipe. Then he remembered that he had a torch in his pocket, so he took it out and flashed it down the hole. He saw the gleam of the dog's eyes quite clearly. The dog whined when it saw the light.

I believe it's just frightened, thought Tom. *It doesn't dare to go backwards or forwards. I'll tell Mr Tucker the milkman. Perhaps he can help me.*

He ran through the shed into the dairy and called Mr Tucker, who was there. Together they went back and looked down the pipe.

'Have you got a bone or something?' asked Tom. 'If you have, we might put it on a bit of string and throw it down the pipe. Then the dog would smell it and perhaps come up after it!'

'That's a good idea!' said the milkman. He went into his house next door to the dairy and fetched a big bone. Tom tied it on to a piece of string and then threw the bone down the pipe. The dog smelt it and whined eagerly, for it was hungry. It began to struggle upwards, and Tom laughed in delight.

'My trick's working!' he said. 'He's coming all right! Good dog, good dog!'

The dog got almost to the pipe opening and then seemed to get stuck again. Tom had pulled the bone away as the dog got nearer to it, for he wanted the animal to come right up to the opening. Now he untied the string and left the bone by the pipe opening.

'I believe I could put my hand in and reach him now,' said Tom. So he lay down on the pavement, put in his arm and felt about for the dog's collar. He took hold of it and tugged. The dog came out with a rush – and there he was on the pavement beside Tom, eagerly gnawing the bone!

'Good!' said the milkman, looking down at him. 'What a nice little dog! I wonder who it belongs to. I'll look at his collar and see.'

Just then the church clock struck two! Tom jumped – and looked down at his clothes. 'Two o'clock!' he said. 'I'm supposed to be at school – we're going to the circus, and look at the mess I'm in!'

'You certainly do look dirty,' said Mr Tucker. 'Your clothes are all dusty, and your hair is in a dreadful mess too. Come indoors and get yourself clean.'

'Oh, I can't do that,' said Tom. 'I shall be too late. I must go as I am.'

'All right,' said the milkman. 'I'll take the dog

back to his owner. Hurry, now, or you'll be too late for the circus.'

Tom rushed off, thinking that perhaps he might have time to wash at school – but as he slipped in, he saw his class marching into the big hall. His teacher caught sight of him and beckoned him to take his place at once.

Poor Tom! He took his place in the line, hot, dirty and untidy. And, most unfortunately, his class were right at the front, just by the platform on which the headmaster stood. Tom ran his hand over his hair to make it straight, and rubbed his face with his handkerchief. He did hope the headmaster would not look at him.

'Now, you are all here, I hope,' said the headmaster pleasantly. 'And how clean and tidy you look – really I feel proud of you! Hair well-brushed, clothes all tidy, faces clean ... but wait a moment! *Who* is this boy in front?'

Of course, it was poor Tom! There he stood,

blushing red.

'Come out!' said the headmaster in an awful voice. Tom stood out.

'What is this I see?' said the headmaster, looking Tom up and down. 'Dirty hands – black knees and unwashed face – scruffy clothes – hair anyhow! How DARE you come to school like this after what I have said?'

'Sir, I f-f-found a dog in a pipe,' began Tom, but the headmaster frowned so much that he stopped, afraid to go on.

'I have heard what a dirty little boy you always are,' said the headmaster sternly. 'Well, this time you shall be punished. You will stay here by yourself and write out *I must keep clean* one hundred times in your best writing. I will NOT take a ragamuffin like you to the circus.'

Tom went to his classroom, his eyes full of tears. He was very unhappy indeed – and a good many tears dropped on to his book when he heard the sound of the other children walking down the street to the circus. It was to begin at three o'clock. How he wished he could be there!

But I'm not sorry I got that dog out, he thought. *I just had to do that. I couldn't leave it. I never thought about getting dirty.*

Now the milkman had looked at the dog's collar, and to his surprise he saw printed on it: *Toby, Miller's Circus*.

'Why, it's a circus dog!' he said in astonishment. 'I'd better take him back at once. He may be wanted this afternoon for all I know. Perhaps he is a performing dog.'

So he put the dog on a lead and took him to the gate that led into the circus field. He told the man there about the dog, and he was at once taken to a caravan behind the tents.

'Hey, Joe!' called the gate man. 'Here's someone with your dog! Just in time too!' A man looked out of the caravan. He had the white face of a clown, and was dressed in clown's clothes. When he saw the dog he gave a whoop of delight, and ran down the caravan steps at once.

'Why, Toby, Toby boy!' he said. 'Where have you been? I was getting so worried about you.' Then he turned to the milkman. 'That's the cleverest dog in the circus!' he said. 'He always performs with me – and the things he does! He is a clown dog, I always say. I didn't know what I was going to do without him, I can tell you! I am much obliged to you for bringing him. Would you like free tickets for the circus?'

'Well,' said the milkman, 'you oughtn't really to thank me. I didn't get him for you. He was down a drainpipe under my shed, and a small boy found him there and got him out by means of a bone on a string. Your dog had got stuck there through fright or something. He might have been there for days if young Tom Allen hadn't found him.'

'Well, I'll have to go and thank him then,' said the clown. 'I expect he'll be with all the schoolchildren at the circus this afternoon, won't he? There they are, look, in the seats over there – just sitting down in them.'

The milkman looked. 'I can't see young Tom,' he said. 'But I expect he'll be there. Look, that's the headmaster. If you go and ask him, he'll tell you which boy is Tom Allen. Now I must go. Goodbye – and good luck to the show!'

Off went Mr Tucker. The clown finished dressing himself, and then dressed Toby the dog in a clown's costume too. At once the little dog began to prance about and behave very comically. He knew quite well that the circus was about to begin!

'Come on, Toby, we'll go and find your rescuer now,' said the clown. So with Toby jumping beside him he walked into the ring and up to the headmaster, who was sitting in the front row.

'Good afternoon, sir,' said the clown. 'Would you mind telling me which of your boys is Tom Allen? He rescued my dog from a drainpipe this afternoon, so

I've been told – and I've got him back just in time for the show! I'd like to thank the boy who got him out of the pipe.'

'Tom Allen!' said the master. 'Why, we left him behind – he came to school so dirty and untidy that I couldn't bring him.'

'I suppose he got like that getting Toby out of the pipe,' said the clown. 'Well, it's rather hard that because he helped someone belonging to the circus, he's not allowed to come and see it!'

'I'd no idea that was what he had been doing,' said the headmaster. 'Is that so, really? Well, we must see what can be done. Perhaps he could come tomorrow.'

'Look here, sir, there are ten minutes still before we begin,' said the clown. 'Will you let me go and get the boy? It won't take me more than five minutes on my bike. I don't like to think of him there all alone when he did such a good turn for my dog!'

'Very well,' said the headmaster. 'I don't like to think of it either – poor Tom! Go to the school, and tell him I know all about it and that he can come back with you!'

Off went Joe the clown. He got his bike and was soon pedalling away up the street to the school. He was there in three minutes and ran in at the door.

Tom was still writing out *I must keep clean* when he heard the sound of footsteps going in and out of the classrooms. He wondered who it was – and he was even more surprised when he saw a circus clown coming in at the door! He sat and stared as if he couldn't believe his eyes.

'Hallo,' said the clown. 'Are you Tom Allen? Well, young fellow-me-lad, you're to come along with me! It was my dog you got out of the pipe – and when I went to ask the headmaster which of his boys you were he told me he'd left you here! And when I told him about my dog he sent me to find you and bring you to the circus after all. So get your cap and hurry. Do you want to wash first? You look a bit dirty.'

Tom gave a loud shout of joy and rushed to the

cloakroom to wash himself. It didn't take him long. The clown brushed his clothes for him, and then Tom stood on the bicycle step and the clown rode swiftly back to the circus taking the small boy with him.

It had just begun. All the performers were walking into the ring, and a man was beating an enormous drum. The schoolchildren were clapping madly.

'I must leave you now,' said the clown. 'Go to the headmaster and tell him I've fetched you. Hope you enjoy the show! Come round to my caravan afterwards and see me. Ask for Joey.'

He ran off, and soon was capering about the ring with the other clowns, his dog Toby jumping beside him, falling over whenever his master fell and behaving just like a little clown dog!

Tom made his way through the children and came up to his headmaster. He stood behind his seat, and at last the Head turned and saw him.

'Hallo, it's you, Tom,' he said. 'So the clown fetched you as he said. Well, it was all a mistake. For once in a way you really couldn't help being dirty, could you? Sit down here beside me and join us.'

How they laughed at the clowns, and cheered the beautiful horses dancing in time to the music, and stared in wonder at the acrobats. It was the finest circus you could imagine – and how glad Tom was that he was not left behind at school writing out *I must keep clean* a hundred times!

'Thank you for my seat, sir, and for sending Joey to get me,' said Tom at the end. 'And, sir – I will try to look a bit cleaner in future! I won't let you down again!'

'I take your word for it!' said the Head, and patted him on the shoulder. 'Now, I suppose you want to go and say goodbye to your friend the clown, don't you? Well, hurry off, and see you come clean to school tomorrow morning!'

Tom shot off, and found his way to the caravan where Joey sat eating an enormous tea of shrimps, new bread and iced cake. He was pleased to see Tom.

'Sit down,' he said. 'Have some tea? Go on – there's plenty. Toby and I are pleased to share anything with a boy like you! We won't forget things in a hurry – will we, Toby?'

'Wuff!' said Toby, and wagged his tail.

'You can come to the circus each day we are here,' said the clown generously. 'Tell the man at the gate that you are Joey's friend, and he'll let you in. See!'

'Oh, thank you very much indeed,' said Tom, delighted. 'I say – I am lucky! I thought when I was left behind this afternoon that I wasn't going to go to the circus at all – and I've been after all – and I'll go every day as well!'

'Ah, you never know your luck,' said Joey wisely. 'The best thing is to do what you can for others – and sure enough, others will do what they can for you! Isn't that right, Toby dog?'

And Toby wagged his tail hard and said, 'Wuff!' – so Joey must have been right!

Sulky Susan

SUSAN WAS a sulky little girl. You know what sulky means, don't you? It's when you are cross and won't smile or talk nicely and your mouth turns down instead of up.

Well, Susan was nearly always like that. Everyone called her Sulky Susan. 'Susan's in the sulks again!' her friends said, when they saw her mouth turning down. 'Look at her! Poor old Susan!'

One day an old man met Susan running down the lane. She didn't look where she was going and she bumped into him, bang! He was quite astonished, and so was Susan.

'Little girl, you should really look where you are going,' said the old man. 'You might have hurt yourself and me too.'

Now any other child would have said, 'Oh, I'm so sorry. I'll look next time.'

But not Susan! Oh, no! She didn't say a word, but just went into one of her sulks. She stared up at the old man, her mouth sulky and her forehead one big frown.

'Bless us all!' said the old man, laughing. 'Where did you get that dreadful face, little girl?'

That made Susan sulk even more – and then she saw something that made her heart begin to beat rather fast.

The old man had pointed ears – and behind his glasses his eyes shone green. Susan knew enough fairy tales to know that this old man wasn't an ordinary fellow. No, he must belong to the fairy folk. She had better be careful!

She was just going to run away when the old man took her arm. She tried to wriggle off but it was no use. 'Now I'd just like you to meet someone,' he said in a very pleasant voice. 'Come along. She lives not far away.'

Susan had to go with him. He turned down a funny crooked street that Susan had never seen before and knocked on the door of a house. A girl about fourteen years old opened the door.

Susan thought she had a most unpleasant face. She frowned at them, and spoke in a sharp voice, 'What do you want?'

'Only to see you for a moment,' said the old man. 'Susan, dear – this is Susan Hill, aged fourteen. Do you like her?'

Now Susan Hill was Susan's own name. Wasn't it strange? Susan stared at the big girl and thought she was simply horrid. She looked so very cross. She had pretty hair, golden like Susan's, and a dimple in her chin too, just like Susan's. Her nose was larger than Susan's but it was just the same shape. In fact, she might have been Susan's bigger sister.

'Well, if you have finished staring at me, I'll shut the door,' said Susan Hill in a cross voice, and she slammed the door hard.

The old man turned to Susan. 'Did you like her?' he asked.

'Not a bit,' said Susan, still sulking.

'Well, there's someone else I'd like you to meet too,' said the old man, and he took Susan down another street. He called to a young woman who was hanging out clothes in a garden. She was about twenty-one, and from the back she looked pretty and young, for she had fine yellow hair that was like a golden mist round her head.

The old man called to her, 'Come and meet a little friend of mine.'

The young woman turned – and what a shock Susan got. She wasn't at all pretty from the front, because her face was so sulky and cross. Her mouth turned down and she had three wrinkles across her pretty forehead.

'This young woman is called Susan Hill,' said the

old man to little Susan. 'Shake hands.'

'I haven't time to waste bothering with children!' said the young woman crossly. 'I've all these things to peg up on the line.' Susan stared at the cross young woman, puzzled. She was so like the young girl she had seen, but older – and her name was Susan Hill too. How funny!

'Do you like her?' asked the old man.

'No,' said Susan. 'She's so cross-looking. I thought she was going to be so pretty and nice from the back, but from the front she was horrid.'

'You're right,' said the old man.

'There seem to be a lot of people living about here with the same name as mine,' said Susan. 'Are there any more?'

'I can show you two more if you like,' said the old man. 'Look, here comes one!'

Down the street came a rather large and ugly woman. She would not have been so ugly if only she had smiled, because her hair was so pretty and soft round her face, and there was a dimple in her chin that could have gone in and out when she smiled. But she really was a most unpleasant woman, for she had lines from her nose to her chin, her mouth was turned right down and she frowned all the time. Susan thought she was horrid.

'It's funny that none of the Susan Hills are married,' she said.

'Not so very funny really,' said the old man. 'Nobody likes sulky people, or unkind people, do they? So why should anyone want to marry them? *I* wouldn't.'

Susan began to feel a little uncomfortable. She thought that all this was very strange indeed. She wished she could go home.

'Where is the other Susan Hill?' she asked, after they had walked a good way.

'There she is, coming along tap-tap-tapping with a stick!' said the old man. Susan looked – and, dear me, she nearly ran away in alarm! A most cross-looking old dame was coming along the road. Her face was thin and wrinkled, her mouth was cross and her eyes had almost disappeared under the wrinkles that had come with frowning.

'That's Susan Hill,' said the old man. 'How do you like yourself all through your life, Susan? It is yourself you have been looking at, you know . . . Susan Hill aged fourteen. Susan Hill aged twenty-one. Susan Hill aged forty-five, and Susan Hill aged seventy. Do you think you will like to be her?'

Susan stared at the old man in horror. 'It can't be me!' she cried. 'It can't! Oh, don't let me be like that!'

'*I* can't help you, my child,' said the old man. 'You can only help yourself. You have the prettiest golden hair that is meant to frame a smiling face. You have blue eyes that should twinkle, and a pretty mouth that should turn up and not down. And you have a dimple in your chin that should always be there, all your life. You make your own face, you know. Look at yours in the glass and see what it is like now!'

Susan looked up at the old man's green eyes, twinkling behind his glasses – and then a very strange thing happened. She wasn't looking into those green eyes – she was looking into her own eyes! She was in her own bedroom, looking into her own little mirror.

She saw her sulky face. She saw her eyes drooping at the corners. She saw her cross mouth turning down. She saw a very ugly little girl. 'Now let's see the difference when I smile!' said Susan to herself. So she smiled into the glass.

And the ugly child turned into a pretty one at once! The blue eyes lit up and shone. The dimple danced in and out. The frown went. The mouth curved upwards and showed Susan's pretty white teeth.

It's like magic! thought Susan. *Just like magic. My own magic. That old man said I could make my own face – and I will make it too! I'll make it sweet and smiling, happy and pretty – not like those dreadful Susan Hills he showed me. And I'll begin from this very, very minute!*

So downstairs danced Susan, smiling all over her

face. Her mother was too surprised to speak for a moment. Then she cried out in pleasure, 'What's happened to you, child? I've never seen you look so sweet before!'

Well, I saw Susan yesterday, and she's a darling, with her twinkling eyes and her upturned mouth. And she'll still be a darling, no matter how old she grows. I hope you will too! Go and look into the mirror when you are wearing a sulky face – and smile at yourself. You *will* be astonished at the magical change!

The Magic Biscuits

The Magic Biscuits

CATHY AND John were skipping home through the woods when they saw a little paper bag lying by a tree.

'Look,' said Cathy, stopping. 'There's a bag, and it looks as if it's full of something.'

'Perhaps someone has dropped it,' said John.

'Let's see what's inside,' said Cathy. So the children ran to the bag and Cathy picked it up.

'Ooh!' she said. 'It's full of biscuits. Look, John!'

'They are letter biscuits!' said John. And so they were. Each little biscuit was made like a letter. There were A's and B's and C's – they were really the most exciting little biscuits.

'Aren't they lovely!' said Cathy. 'I wonder who they belong to.'

'We'd better take them along with us and see if we find anyone looking for them,' said John.

So Cathy carried the bag – but how she peeped and peeped into it – and how she longed to nibble some of those dear little biscuits!

'I'm so hungry, John,' she said. 'Do you suppose I might eat just *one* biscuit?'

'Certainly not,' said John. 'They don't belong to us, Cathy. You know Mother wouldn't like us to do a thing like that.'

'But no one would know if I ate one or two,' said Cathy.

'You would know yourself,' said John. 'It's not nice to know you've done something mean.'

'Well, I don't care,' said Cathy. 'I'm just *going* to eat some! Look – here's a C for Cathy!'

She took out a letter C, and popped it into her mouth. She crunched it up – it was delicious.

'I think you're naughty,' said John. Cathy took no notice. She put her hand into the bag again.

'I shall eat my name,' she said. 'I've eaten the letter C – now I want A!'

She found an A and ate that too. Really, the biscuits were the very nicest she had ever tasted! John longed to have one too, but he wouldn't. It was bad enough having a sister who took what wasn't hers!

'Now I want the letter T,' said Cathy, and she hunted about for a T. 'I've had a C and an A; T comes next in my name.'

She found a letter T and put it into her mouth. She crunched it up and swallowed it. John walked on crossly.

'Miaow!' suddenly came a voice. 'Miaow!'

John looked round in amazement. Where the cat?

He soon saw it – a big golden-furred cat that ran after him and mewed.

'Cathy, look at this cat!' called John, looking for his sister – but Cathy had disappeared! She just simply wasn't there. Wherever could she have gone? The bag of biscuits lay on the ground – but Cathy was quite gone.

'Miaow, miaow, miaow!' said the golden cat, and purred and rubbed herself against John's legs. John bent down to stroke her – and looked into the cat's eyes. They were as blue as his sister Cathy's!

'Oh, dear, oh, dear!' said John in a fright. 'Have you turned into a cat, Cathy?'

'Miaow, miaow!' said the cat sadly.

John stared at her. She had fur as golden as Cathy's hair, and eyes as blue as Cathy's. Cathy had certainly changed into a cat! But why?

'It must be those biscuits!' groaned poor John. 'They must be magic ones – but why should they turn Cathy into a cat?'

He soon knew! Cathy had wanted to eat her name in the biscuits – and she had got as far as C-a-t – and the magic in the biscuits had worked, and turned her into what C-A-T spelt! Cat! Whatever was John to do?

'Oh, why did I let Cathy eat those biscuits?' said John. 'I knew it was wrong. Cathy, Cathy, you are a lovely golden cat now – but I want you to be my sister, not a cat.'

The little boy picked up the bag of biscuits and looked all around. If only he could find out who they belonged to! Perhaps the owner would help him, and turn Cathy back to her right shape again. He walked on between the trees and at last came to a small yellow cottage that he was sure he had never seen before. With the cat at his heels he walked up the path and knocked at the door.

'Come in!' called a voice. John opened the door and looked inside. He saw a bent old gnome there, stirring something in a big black pot over the fire.

'Good morning,' said John.

'Morning,' said the gnome, turning round and

blinking at John. 'What do you want? Are you selling anything?'

'No,' said John. 'I just wondered if you knew who these biscuits belonged to.'

'Of course I don't,' said the gnome, who didn't seem to be in a very good temper. 'I like the look of that cat of yours, though – beautiful creature, she is! I'll buy her from you!'

'Oh, no,' said John, alarmed. 'You can't have her. She belongs to me.'

'Here's a piece of gold for her,' said the gnome, and pushed a large piece of gold into John's hand. 'Go on your way now. The cat is mine!'

And, to John's horror, the gnome pushed him out of the cottage and slammed the door in his face. The cat was left behind in the house! Poor Cathy!

'Miaow! Miaow!' she cried, and tried to get out – but the door and the window were both shut.

John banged at the door – but it was locked. He couldn't think *what* to do. He still had the bag of biscuits in his hand. If only he could find the owner and get some help! The little boy wandered off again, hoping he would meet someone.

And at last he did. He met an old, old woman, bent double under a pile of sticks which she was taking home for firewood. She had a red face and twinkling eyes, and she looked so kind that John ran to ask her help.

'Do you know anyone who has dropped a bag of biscuits?' he asked.

The old woman shook her head. 'Could you help me with this bundle of wood?' she said. 'You look a strong boy. I'll carry the biscuits for you.'

So John took the wood from her and walked beside her until they came to a tiny house under a tree – so tiny that John really wondered if there could be room inside to live!

The old woman took the wood and thanked John. 'Why do you look so miserable?' she asked. 'You look as if you've *lost* some biscuits – not found some!'

'I think they must be magic biscuits,' said John, and he showed her them. 'They have turned my sister into a cat.'

'Stars and moon!' said the old dame in surprise. 'Did they really? Let me have a look at these wonderful biscuits. Yes – they are magic all right. I can tell by the smell of them.'

'You see, my sister was eating her name in the letters – her name's Cathy – and she got as far as C-A-T and she turned into a big golden cat,' said John. 'I don't know what to do about it now, because an old gnome in a cottage gave me a piece of gold for her, and kept her. He pushed me out of the cottage and I had to leave Cathy behind.'

'He had no right to do that!' said the old woman. 'I know him – mean old thing he is too! Now let me think a bit, little boy. I'm not a witch or anybody very clever, but I've lived among fairy folk all my life and know their ways.'

She sat down on the low wall outside her tiny

house and looked at the biscuits.

'So, Cathy turned into a cat because she ate C-A-T!' she said. 'Well, little boy, listen – suppose you creep back to the cottage and give the cat two more letters, H and Y, to finish her name. Perhaps she will change back to Cathy then! What a shock for the gnome!'

'Ooh! That's a good idea!' said John, pleased. 'I didn't think of that! I'll go back to the cottage at once, and see if I can give Cathy the other two biscuits to finish her name!'

So off he went back to the gnome's cottage. The window was now the smallest bit open at the bottom. John peeped in. The gnome was drying his hands on a towel at the other end of the kitchen. Cathy was lying down on a mat, mewing.

'Cathy!' whispered John. 'Eat these two biscuits quickly – the H first and then the Y. Hurry!'

The big golden cat ran up to the window. John dropped two letter biscuits inside – an H and a Y. Cathy pounced on them and chewed them up.

And, no sooner had she eaten them than she shot up into a little girl again! There she was, the same golden-haired, blue-eyed Cathy, *so* pleased to be herself again.

The gnome turned round and saw her. He *was* surprised. 'What are *you* doing here in my cottage!' he cried. 'Go out at once!'

That was just what Cathy was longing to do! She ran to the door, unlocked it and raced down the path to John. How glad she was to be with him again!

'Quick! Let's go home!' she said. They ran quickly through the wood, found the right path and raced home at top speed.

'Mother! Mother!' cried John. 'Where are you? We've had such an adventure! Cathy got turned into a cat. She ate some magic biscuits.'

They told Mother all about it, and Mother was most astonished. 'Let me see these magic biscuits,' she said. 'This is a wonderful story.'

But John hadn't got them! He had left them behind

in the wood. Wasn't it a pity? And when he went to find them the next day they had gone.

'I expect the right owner found them,' he said to Cathy. 'I wonder if he'll notice that five of the biscuits are gone.'

'I shan't do a thing like that again,' said Cathy. 'It was horrid, being a cat! But it was nice having a tail to wave about, John.'

'I don't want you to be a cat again,' said John.

I don't expect Cathy ever will be, do you?

The Boy Who Made Faces

The Boy Who
Made Faces

WILLIE WAS a very good-looking little boy, and his mother was proud of him. She didn't know how ugly he looked when she wasn't there.

He pulled faces. He made faces to frighten the little girls. He made faces behind the teacher's back at school just to feel clever. He made faces at other people just to be rude.

He screwed up his nose. He squinted. He blew out his cheeks. And when he wanted to be very rude he put out his tongue. The little girls were really frightened of him, especially when he rolled his eyes round and round and round.

'One day, Willie, the wind will change when you are making a face,' said old Mrs Lambie. 'And then your face will get stuck. You are a very rude little boy. I only wish your father knew the rude faces you make at me and at other people you meet.'

Willie didn't like Mrs Lambie. He squinted at her and put out his tongue, and then he ran away. He really was a very rude little boy.

'Pooh! Fancy telling me that old story about my face getting stuck if the wind changes,' said Willie, and he laughed. 'What a lot of nonsense!'

And then something happened. It happened that very afternoon, as Willie was going home from school. He passed the old man who sold newspapers at the corner and, as he always did, he put his tongue out at him. In and out went his tongue, in and out, and Willie danced around as he made his face.

The wind changed suddenly. One moment it was blowing from the west, the next moment it dropped – and then it blew again from the east . . .

And Willie's face was stuck! He squinted, and his tongue went in and out! He didn't notice it at first as he ran off squinting, his tongue going in and out rudely.

'Oh, dear, I've squinted too hard and my eyes won't come right,' said Willie suddenly. 'And why won't my tongue keep in? Goodness, here comes my headmaster. I'd better cross to the other side of the road.'

But his headmaster called to him, 'Good afternoon, Willie. Hurry along home.'

To Willie's horror his red tongue came out and waggled itself at the headmaster, who looked most astonished and annoyed. Before he could say a word, Willie, as red as a beetroot, tore down the road and disappeared round a corner.

He was beginning to feel very worried. He still couldn't see very well because his eyes were squinting just as much, and it was very, very difficult for him to keep his tongue in his mouth, even if he dug his teeth into it.

He slipped indoors. His mother called to him, 'Willie, you're late! Wash and then come to tea.'

Willie washed. He had managed to keep his tongue in his mouth for a little while, but he didn't know how long it would remain tucked inside his mouth. He sidled into the dining room, not looking at his mother.

He began his tea, and his tongue was soon so busy helping his teeth to eat that Willie forgot about it. He looked at his mother when she spoke to him – and out went his tongue! His mother gazed at him in horror.

'Willie! What are you putting your tongue out at me for? And oh, don't squint like that! Willie, do you hear me? Don't be such a rude, silly little boy!'

But that tongue waggled away, and his mother got up sharply. She took Willie from his chair, and sent him out of the room.

Soon his father came home looking angry. 'Where's Willie?' he said. 'I met his headmaster when I was out, and he told me that Willie actually made faces at him when he met him in the road. I can't have that. Where is he?'

'He's upstairs,' said Willie's mother. 'I sent him out of the room for making faces at me. Whatever has come over him?'

'Well, whatever it is, I'll soon change him!' said Willie's father, and he went up to find Willie. The boy heard him coming, and in a panic he got into bed, clothes and all, and pulled the sheet halfway over his face.

Oh, I hope I don't put my tongue out at Daddy! he thought. *Oh, dear, this is dreadful. I must keep my teeth tightly closed, then my tongue won't come out.*

His father came in. 'Willie,' he said, 'what is this I hear from your headmaster? Did you really pull faces at him? Have you gone mad?'

Willie shook his head, not daring to unclose his teeth to speak, in case his tongue popped out.

'Answer me properly, yes or no,' said his father

angrily. 'Shaking your head like that! And what are you squinting for?'

'Oh, Daddy,' began poor Willie, but he got no further because out popped his tongue and waggled itself at his astonished father.

Well, quite a lot of things happened to Willie after that, because his father didn't allow boys to behave rudely to him and scolded him.

'That's for being rude to your headmaster, to your mother and to me,' said his father. 'Now let me see if your tongue is better.'

Well, whether the wind changed again at that moment or not, I don't know, but certainly Willie's tongue behaved itself after that. Maybe it was as frightened as poor Willie! But the dreadful thing was that his eyes didn't come right, and he still squinted.

So now he has to wear glasses till they get right, and he doesn't like it a bit. He does wish he had never pulled such silly faces.

The Tell-Tale Bird

The Tell-Tale Bird

THERE WAS once a little girl called Tilly, who told tales all day long. I don't like tell-tales, do you? Well, nobody liked Tilly!

'Mummy, Peter pushed me today! Mummy, Ann dirtied her frock! Mummy, Pussy has been lying on your best cushion! Mummy, the postman dropped one of your letters in the mud and dirtied it – I saw him!'

That was how Tilly told tales all the day, and people got so cross with her! Ah, but wait! She didn't know the tell-tale bird was about!

It came one day and flew in at Tilly's window as she brushed her hair before breakfast. It was a blue and yellow bird with rather a long tail. And it looked very queer because it had ears! No bird has ears like those that animals have, but this bird had feathery ones on each side of its head.

'Shoo!' said Tilly, waving her brush at the bird. 'Shoo! Go away! Birds are not allowed in the house.'

'I am!' squawked the bird in a loud voice. 'I am! I'm the tell-tale bird, I am! And I've been looking for a little girl like you for a long time! Yes, a long, long time! I've come to live with you. We ought to be friends, Tilly, for you're a tell-tale girl and I'm a tell-tale bird.'

Tilly didn't know what to make of it all. She decided to tell her mother about the bird when she went downstairs. So down she went – and the bird flew on to her shoulder as she went.

'Mummy, Mummy, this horrid bird flew in at my window!' said Tilly in her usual grumbling voice.

'Tilly didn't brush her hair properly, Tilly didn't brush her hair properly!' squawked the bird, jumping up and down on Tilly's shoulder in a most annoying way.

'Why, it's a tell-tale bird!' said Mummy in surprise. 'I didn't think there were any left nowadays. Well, Tilly, you'll have to put up with it, I'm afraid, for as long as you tell tales the bird will want to stay with you and be friends.'

Tilly pushed it off her shoulder angrily. 'Nasty thing!' she said. 'Get away! I won't have you here.'

The bird flew to the electric light and swung there on the cord.

'Tilly's got dirty nails!' he squawked. 'Tilly's got dirty nails!'

Tilly was sent to scrub her nails. The bird went with her. The little girl banged the door and wouldn't let the bird come in. But it flew down the stairs, out of the door and in at the bedroom window. So Tilly had to put up with it.

They went downstairs again together, the bird on Tilly's shoulder. It dug its claws in if Tilly tried to push it off, so she decided it had better stay. But she didn't mean it to come to school with her. Oh, dear, no!

They had breakfast. The tell-tale bird had very bad manners and often snatched at something that Tilly was just going to put into her mouth. It made her jump too, whenever it gave a loud squawk, which it always seemed to be doing.

'Tilly's spilt her milk!' squawked the bird in delight, when it saw Tilly spill a tiny little drop. 'Dirty girl! She's a dirty girl!'

'You horrid tell-tale!' said Tilly nearly in tears.

'Tilly's hidden her crust under her plate!' squawked the bird in a little while. 'She's a naughty girl!'

'It's only because I've got two teeth loose and I can't chew properly!' cried Tilly in a rage.

'Well, say so then,' said her daddy. 'Don't hide things and hope we won't notice. That is not at all a brave thing to do.'

'Tilly's a coward, a coward, a coward!' screamed the bird joyously. Tilly got up from the table in tears, and said she was going to get ready for school. The bird went with her. As soon as they were upstairs, Tilly got hold of the bird and pushed it into her toy cupboard. She locked the door, got her hat and tore off to school without even kissing Mummy goodbye. That shows how upset she was!

She was so glad to be rid of the horrid tell-tale bird. She took her place in her class and opened her books. It was sums. She peeped over at the next child's book.

'Billy's got a sum down all wrong, Miss Brown,' she said. 'He's copied it out wrong.'

There was a squawk at the window. There sat the tell-tale bird, its ears cocked up at each side of its head! It had made such a noise in the toy cupboard that Mummy had had to let it out – and it had flown joyfully off to school. As soon as it got there and heard Tilly telling tales as usual, it knew it had found the right little girl.

'Tilly's got a hole in her stocking!' squawked the bird, jigging up and down in delight. 'I saw it this morning. And she had to be sent back at breakfast time to brush her hair again and scrub her dirty nails!'

Tilly went red. The other children giggled. 'Good gracious!' said Miss Brown. 'A tell-tale bird! I haven't seen one for a very long time. Does it belong to you, Tilly?'

'No,' said Tilly in a rude voice.

'Oh, I do, I do!' cried the bird, flying to Tilly's shoulder and nuzzling its head against her cheek. 'I'm Tilly's tell-tale bird! She's a lovely tell-tale! I love her, I do!'

'Well, do you mind sitting on the mantelpiece for a bit?' asked Miss Brown. 'I really don't think Tilly can work properly with you on her shoulder.'

'Oh, with pleasure!' cried the bird, and it flew to the mantelpiece, where it looked in a kindly manner at everyone in the class. It was really a most extraordinary bird.

The class worked hard. Suddenly the little boy beside Tilly whispered to the little girl on his other side. At once Tilly put up her hand.

'Miss Brown, Billy's talking and you said we weren't to!' she said.

Miss Brown was just going to say, 'Don't tell tales!' when the tell-tale bird gave a tremendously loud squawk and cried, 'Tilly's got ink on her fingers! Tilly's got ink on her fingers! Dirty girl! Dirty girl!'

'Be quiet, you horrid creature!' cried Tilly, trying to rub the ink off her fingers.

'Well, Tilly, you can't blame the bird for doing what you do all day long,' said Miss Brown. 'You tell tales – and the bird does too! It is only doing what you do.'

Nothing more happened till the children went out to play. The bird went to sleep with its head under its wing. Tilly was glad. The children went out into the garden and the bird woke up and went too. Soon Tilly came running in.

'Miss Brown, Miss Brown, Tommy pushed Eileen over! And Dick pulled my hair! And Alice dropped her cake on the ground and then picked it up and ate the dirty pieces—'

The tell-tale bird flew on to Tilly's shoulder and flapped its wings in her face.

'Miss Brown, Miss Brown!' it cried in a voice very like Tilly's. 'Tilly pushed Leslie! And she trod on George's toe on purpose – I saw her! And she fell down and dirtied her clean dress!'

'Dear me!' said Miss Brown. 'Well, Tilly, if I listen to your tales, I must listen to the bird's too.'

'You're not to listen to the horrid tales the bird tells!' cried Tilly, and she rushed out crying. She made up her mind not to tell a single tale more that morning. The funny thing is that she didn't! The bird went to sleep again, its head under its wing. School was very happy and peaceful.

Tilly ran home, leaving the bird fast asleep on the mantelpiece. Nobody seemed to remember it, not even Miss Brown. Tilly was pleased. She washed her hands, brushed her hair and sat down at the dinner table.

'Well, did you have a nice morning, Tilly?' asked Mummy.

'Yes,' said Tilly. 'But a lot of the children were naughty, Mummy. Billy copied his sum wrong, and Alice got her spelling wrong, and—'

The tell-tale bird suddenly flew in at the window with such a loud squawk that Tilly dropped her spoon in fright.

'Here we are again!' said the bird, cocking its feathery ears up straight. 'Tilly fell down and dirtied her dress at playtime! Tilly got ink on her fingers! Tilly told tales! Tilly—'

'Be quiet!' shouted Tilly, and she threw her spoon at the bird. It caught it neatly on its beak, and then flew to the table. It dipped the spoon into Tilly's plate of meat, potato and gravy and began to eat solemnly. Tilly was so angry.

'Now listen, Tilly,' said her mother. 'You will have to put up with the tell-tale bird. It only comes to people who tell tales, and it is your own fault that it has come to you. Stop telling tales, and the bird will soon go somewhere else!'

'I'll never tell another tale in my life!' wept Tilly.

But although she had made up her mind about this, she found it was much more difficult than she had thought. She was such a dreadful little tell-tale that it was very difficult for her to stop suddenly.

Whenever she forgot and told a tale, the tell-tale bird was delighted and at once shouted out a whole lot of things about Tilly!

'Tilly lost her hair ribbon yesterday! Tilly got scolded this morning for being rude! Tilly had to stay in at school for getting her sums wrong! Tilly broke a cup at teatime! Tilly's a baby, she spilt her cocoa down her front!'

So the bird went on, and there was no way of stopping it at all, except by Tilly never telling a tale herself. In about a month Tilly had stopped telling tales. She always thought twice before she spoke now, and became a much nicer little girl. The other children began to like her. She was asked out to tea and made a lot of friends.

And one day the tell-tale bird flew away! It squawked for the last time on the mantelpiece, 'You're no good at telling tales now, Tilly! I'm going to look for someone else! It's no fun here now!' And it spread its blue and yellow wings, flew out of the window and disappeared.

I'm not quite sure where it went to – but if you hear people say, 'Ah, a little bird told me!' you may be sure that tell-tale bird is somewhere about, telling tales and secrets just as it did when it was with Tilly!

Porridge Town

THERE WAS once a little boy called James, who was very messy with his porridge at breakfast time. He liked to stir it round and round in his plate, and then it always went over the edge on to the cloth.

'James! You've dirtied the clean tablecloth again!' cried his mother almost every day. 'Oh, dear, if only you would try and eat your porridge up properly instead of getting it on the floor and on the table!'

After James had finished his breakfast each morning, Mummy had to take a cloth and wipe up porridge spots on the carpet, dropped off James's spoon, and she had to wipe up plenty of messes on the cloth as well.

One morning Mummy was very cross with James because he had made a bigger mess than usual.

'Now, James! I am going to get a cloth to wipe up that mess,' she said, 'and if your porridge is not finished by the time I come back, you shall not have your nice boiled egg this morning, and you will have to sit in the corner and think about porridge for half an hour!'

Mummy went to get a cloth. Did James eat his porridge up quickly as soon as she had gone? No, he did not! He sat there, dreaming, looking out of the window, stirring his porridge and making some more slop over the edge of his plate. He really was a most annoying child.

Then he heard Mummy coming back, and he remembered what she had said. No egg – and half an hour in the corner if he hadn't emptied his plate of porridge! Well, there certainly wasn't time to eat it. Whatever was he to do?

You will never guess what that naughty boy did! He took up his plate, turned it upside down out of the window and emptied all his porridge into the garden.

He heard an angry yell from below the window, but he hadn't time to look out and see what had happened because Mummy came back. She took a look at his plate and said, 'Oh, so you have managed to eat up your porridge quickly for once. And a good thing too!'

Naughty James didn't say a word. He watched Mummy wipe up the mess he had made, and then he began to eat his egg, wondering who had yelled like that in the garden.

He soon found out when he went to play on the lawn. A fierce little brownie ran out from under the lilac bush and caught hold of him.

'Was it you who poured porridge all over me?' he cried angrily. 'Look at me! It's all over my hair and down my neck! You nasty, horrid boy!'

James looked at the angry little man, and he began to laugh. The brownie had porridge all over his hat and down his neck. He really did look funny.

'Oh! So instead of begging my pardon you think you'll laugh at me, do you!' shouted the brownie, getting crosser and crosser. 'Well, my boy, you just come along with me to Porridge Town! It isn't very far, and maybe you will see then what it is like to have porridge when you don't want it!'

Then, to James's surprise and dismay, he dragged him to the gate, whisked him down a path and through a strange gate that James knew he had never seen before – and before he could say anything, there he was in a crooked little town, with tumbledown houses, twisty chimneys and a crowd of little folk going about their shopping.

'This is Porridge Town,' said the brownie with a grin. 'Have a good time, nasty little boy!'

James didn't like the look of Porridge Town at all.

He wandered along by himself, and came to a seat by the road. He sat down on it. Presently a bus came along, and splashed through a big puddle – and the puddle splashed all over poor James.

And when he looked down to see if his suit had been messed, he found that he was covered all over in porridge!

Yes – all the puddles in the road were full of porridge instead of water. It was most disgusting! Poor James tried to wipe the porridge off himself, but his hanky soon got wet and sticky.

He got up and went on again. He saw some lovely buns in a baker's shop, and he wondered if he had a penny. Yes, he had. So into the shop he went and bought a penny bun.

But, dear me, when he bit into it, what a surprise! The inside was full of porridge that squirted out all over James! Some went down his neck and some went on to his chest.

The little folk who were passing thought it was

a great joke, and they laughed and laughed at him. James was angry and ran away. He fell down – and, of course, he fell into a porridge puddle! He did hate that.

A little old woman came out of a nearby cottage and helped him up. 'Come and rest in my cottage for a minute and I'll tie up your knee,' she said.

So into her house went James and sat down on a nice, fat, soft cushion. And, do you know, it burst under him, and goodness gracious, will you believe it, it was full of porridge!

Well, it is horrid enough to fall down in a porridge puddle, but it is even worse to *sit* in porridge! James got up in a hurry and went out of the cottage at a run. He simply couldn't bear the idea of sitting down in another chair there.

Not far off was a big apple tree and on it were some rosy, ripe apples. It was not the time of year for apples and James was most surprised. He thought he would go and sit under the tree and maybe an apple would fall down by him, and he could eat it.

Well, the apples were very ripe and they did fall down. But they were not like ordinary apples. Oh, no!

One fell on to James's head and burst at once – and as you can guess, it was full of porridge. In fact, it was a porridge-apple! Another one fell down and burst on his shoulder, sending wet porridge down his neck. A third apple fell on his hand, and covered it with porridge too – hot porridge this time, so that James was burnt and sprang up with a shout of pain!

He ran away from that peculiar tree. He ran and he ran. He didn't know where he was going to, but he meant to get away from Porridge Town. He ran fast. It seemed to him as if he ran for miles. And after a while he found himself on a path in a garden, rushing along at top speed.

He bumped into someone. 'What's the hurry?' cried a voice.

'I want to get home!' cried James. 'Tell me the way!'

Then he looked up and saw – his mother! She *was* astonished.

'You *are* at home!' she said. 'Fancy galloping along like this at sixty miles an hour to get home, when you are in your own garden. Really, James!'

'Am I in my own garden? How funny!' cried James. 'I've been all the way to Porridge Town and back, Mother.'

'Well, I hope you didn't make as much mess there as you did at breakfast this morning!' said his mother. James looked down at himself – and to his surprise he was quite clean. He hadn't a scrap of porridge on him. Could he possibly have imagined it all?

But, dear me, when he put his hands into his pockets, what a shock he got! They were full of porridge – hot porridge too! That was the last trick one of the little folk in Porridge Town had managed to play on him. Poor James! He didn't say a word to his mother but hurried off to the bathroom. He turned his pockets inside out and tried his best to sponge out the porridge. And he made up his mind about something.

'I shall eat up my porridge in the morning and not make a single mess!' he said to himself. 'Oh, dear, I really don't think I could *bear* to see a porridge spot on the cloth again!'

Do you make messes? What! You do? Come along to Porridge Town then, and we'll see what happens!

Sally's Silly
Mistake

Sally's Silly Mistake

IT WAS a blowy, blustery April day when Sally set out
to go and call on her Aunt Amanda. She had to hold
on to her hat tightly, or it would have flown straight
off her head.

'Oh, dear, oh, dear – what a wind!' said poor Sally,
struggling along, her skirts blowing this way and
that. She put down her hand to pat her skirts straight
– and at once her hat flew right off her head!

'Look at that now!' said Sally. She turned to watch
the hat bowling along. 'All those pretty flowers on my
hat getting muddy and wet – and the brim getting
bent. And I did so badly want to look nice for Aunt

Amanda. She is so very particular!'

She went after her hat. It was lying in a puddle. She shook the water from it and it flew all over her. 'I can't wear it any more!' she wailed. 'It's spoilt!'

She tucked it under her arm and struggled on again. She felt drops of rain on her head – now it was going to rain hard and soak her through!

The rain came down in bucketfuls. Sally had an umbrella with her, and she shook it out ready to put up. She opened it – and immediately the wind took it and turned it inside out!

Sally could have cried. First her hat spoilt and now her nice umbrella blown inside out. Bother the wind! She put her ruined umbrella under her arm with her hat and walked on again. When she got to the corner of the lane the wind rushed at her with such strength that she was blown backwards – and down she went on the wet grass at the edge of the lane.

She sat there to get her breath, and then she suddenly saw something by her knee. Why – it was a four-leaved clover! Fancy that!

'A four-leaved clover!' cried Sally. 'Now, there's a bit of luck! Anybody knows a four-leaved clover is lucky. And I need good luck too, after all the bad luck I've had this morning with my hat and my umbrella!'

She picked the clover carefully and put it into her bag. Now she would really be lucky. What a pity she hadn't found it before her hat and umbrella had been spoilt.

She went down the lane, on the way to her aunt's, shaking her hat every now and again, hoping it would be all right to wear. But she was sure it wouldn't. The flowers were muddy and torn, and the brim was wet and was coming apart in two places.

It began to rain hard again. Sally stepped off the road and went into a little shed to shelter – and there she saw something very surprising indeed!

A hat was hanging on a nail at the back of the shed and beside it, on another nail, was a neatly rolled umbrella, striped black and red – really a very nice one indeed.

'Well, now, look there!' said Sally, amazed. 'Would you believe it? If that isn't good luck brought by the four-leaved clover already! My, my, I wonder what else I shall find. This is too good to be true!'

She put the pretty flowery hat on her head, and took down the neat umbrella. She hung up her own spoilt hat and put the inside-out umbrella beside it.

Then off she went, feeling very grand. The rain had stopped, and the wind wasn't quite so blowy. But, all the same, Sally held her new hat on tightly.

Aunt Amanda was very pleased to see her. '*What* a pretty new hat, Sally!' she said. 'Do come in. And my, you've a new umbrella too, I see. Leave it in the hall. That's right. You go and wait in the sitting room until I come. I'm just baking a few cakes for tea, because I've a friend coming.'

'That *will* be nice,' said Sally happily. 'It will be quite a party. If you're sure I can't help you, Aunt

Amanda, I'll just go and look round the garden.'

Off she went, and spent a nice time looking at the daffodils and wallflowers and primroses. Then she heard voices from the kitchen, and she guessed her aunt's friend must have arrived.

I'd better go back to the house, thought Sally. So back she went. As she passed the kitchen window she heard her aunt's voice.

'Well, I never did! Whatever do you mean, Mrs Smart? Somebody stole your hat and umbrella? But how did that happen?'

'Well, I was going along the lane in my best hat with my best umbrella,' said the friend's voice loudly, 'and I saw a little lamb in the ditch. So I went to lift it through the hedge – and I took off my new hat first, in case the wind should blow it off my head, and hung it in a nearby shed, and I hung up my best umbrella beside it.'

'And when you came back they were gone!' said Aunt Amanda, shocked. 'You should go to the police, Mrs Smart.'

'They were not only gone, but someone or other had left these awful old things in their place,' said Mrs Smart, showing Aunt Amanda a dreadful hat, wet and muddy, and an inside-out umbrella. 'Did you ever see such things?'

Sally stood outside the window, shaking at the knees. Oh my, oh my! It wasn't a bit of luck she had had after all; it was just that Mrs Smart had put her hat and umbrella carefully out of the way when she went to get the lamb. And she, Sally, had taken them and put her spoilt ones in their place.

Whatever was she to do? She stole into the house and took off the smart new hat. She hung it on a peg in the hall, just above where she had stood the neat umbrella.

Her own spoilt has was there on the peg and the ragged umbrella in a corner nearby. Sally took them with trembling hands.

She must go! Mrs Smart would be so very, very angry if she knew what Sally had done, and Aunt

Amanda would never, never forgive her.

I ought to own up, I know I ought, thought Sally. *But I daren't. Anyway, I'm trying to put things right again. And oh, I know what I'll do! I'll slip my four-leaved clover, my precious four-leaved clover, into the ribbon round Mrs Smart's lovely hat – then she'll get some luck, and I'll have made up to her for being so very silly.*

So she put the four-leaved clover into the hatband. Then she stole out of the front door, wearing her wet, raggedy hat, with her inside-out umbrella under her arm.

Poor Sally – it was a pity she didn't stay and own up. Mrs Smart would have laughed and laughed, and so would Aunt Amanda. And she would have had a lovely tea and felt very much better. But she wasn't brave enough.

I wish I was going to be there when Mrs Smart suddenly sees her own hat and umbrella in the hall, don't you? She *will* get a tremendous surprise! Whatever will she say?

The Astonishing Party

The Astonishing Party

ALL THE children in Hawthorne Village were excited. They had been invited to a party. And Dame Twinkle was giving it! Dame Twinkle was a marvellous person, as magic as can be. She knew all kinds of tricks and jokes and spells. She could tell you what the weather would be on Wednesday week. She could tell you where to find the first violet and the biggest bluebell. She knew where the juiciest blackberries grew and the finest nuts.

She was jolly and friendly and amusing – and how she could scold if she was cross! It would be exciting to go to a party given by Dame Twinkle.

'You'll have to behave yourselves,' said Miss Brown, their teacher. 'Dame Twinkle doesn't like naughty or ill-mannered children, so be careful!'

Well, the children all dressed themselves up nicely and went up the hill to Dame Twinkle's cottage. Its windows were like her name – they twinkled in the sun, and the garden was bright with flowers. It was a sunny day, so the children hoped they could play in the garden.

Dame Twinkle welcomed them. 'Good afternoon, Amy – and Benny – and Connie – and Dick – and Elaine and all of you! How nice you look!'

'I hope she's got a good tea!' whispered Patrick to Connie. Dame Twinkle had sharp ears and she heard what Patrick said. She frowned.

'Now,' she said, 'this will be rather a funny party, so be careful how you behave. There is a good bit of magic about the garden this afternoon!'

First of all Dame Twinkle gave the children coloured balloons to play with. That was fun! They threw them into the air, punched them when they came down again and had a lovely time.

Then Gloria threw her balloon too near a holly bush – and it caught on a prickle and burst. Gloria burst too – into tears! She sobbed and she wailed, and Dame Twinkle came running up in alarm.

'My dear child, what have you done – broken a leg or an arm?'

'My balloon's burst!' wailed Gloria.

'Now, my dear, you are behaving like a little goose,' said Dame Twinkle firmly. And then a very strange thing happened.

Gloria turned into a goose! She did, really. She still wore her own clothes, but she was a goose. She opened her beak to wail, but she cackled instead.

'Oh, it's the magic in the garden!' cried the children in delight. 'Oh, Dame Twinkle, Gloria behaved like a goose and now she is one! Goosie-goosie-Gloria!'

'Well, well, you can't say I didn't warn you!' said Dame Twinkle. 'Cheer up, Gloria, the magic will go sooner or later!'

'Dame Twinkle, do you like the beautiful dress my aunty gave me?' said Polly, a very vain little girl, running up to Dame Twinkle. She twisted herself round to show the dress.

'My!' said Dame Twinkle. 'You're as proud as a peacock, Polly, aren't you!'

And dear me, Polly changed into a peacock! There she stood, dressed in her clothes still, but with a magnificent tail spread out behind her – a very fine peacock indeed. She opened her beak to cry, but made an ugly screeching noise instead.

Micky stared, afraid. He ran into a corner and tried to hide. He was always afraid of everything. Elaine pointed her finger at him. 'Look at Micky! He's as timid as a mouse!'

And Micky at once turned into a mouse, of course – a nice big one, dressed in shorts and jersey, with a woffly nose and a long tail. He had to carry it because he fell over it. He squeaked when he wanted to talk.

'I say, we'd better be careful,' said Connie in alarm. 'There's an awful lot of magic about today!'

'Come and have tea, come and have tea!' cried Dame Twinkle, and the children rushed indoors. They saw such a fine tea, and Patrick's eyes gleamed. He was a very greedy little boy. He sat himself down opposite the biggest plate of buns.

How he ate! He stuffed himself full of buns and sandwiches, cakes and biscuits, and the other children stared at him in disgust.

'You're as greedy as a pig, Patrick,' said Bobby. And dear me – Patrick was immediately a pig! There he sat, grunting, his little piggy eyes staring all round and his curly tail sticking out at the back of him. The children laughed. Patrick really did look very funny.

The children were told to help themselves, and they did – all except Dick, who waited to be asked. Nobody asked him what he wanted, of course, and he felt very hurt, and sat with his plate empty for a long time.

He saw all the other children eating the things he liked. Soon his eyes filled with tears and he cried.

'What's the matter?' said Dame Twinkle. 'Do you feel ill, Dick?'

'No. But, oh, nobody looks after me, nobody offers me anything and I've had hardly any tea!' wailed Dick.

'Well, didn't I tell you all to help yourselves?' said Dame Twinkle impatiently. 'You *are* a little donkey!'

And he was – a dear little grey donkey, with big, long ears that twitched, and a voice that said 'Hee-haw!' very loudly! The other children laughed and petted him.

'Shall I get you some thistles and carrots for your tea?' said John. 'Dear little Dickie Donkey!'

Martin slipped away from the table and went into the field beyond the garden. He came back with an armful of thistles which he pushed under poor Dick's nose.

'Now, Martin, now,' said Dame Twinkle, 'you

really are a monkey to go and get those thistles!'

And of course, as soon as she said that, Martin was a monkey with a grinning face, and a long tail that was very useful to him, for he at once jumped up to the lamp and hung downwards from it by his tail!

The children squealed. What an astonishing party! Who would change next? Really, it was so sudden, you never knew what your neighbour was going to turn into from one minute to the next.

Frank pushed some food into his pocket, hoping that no one would see him. Then he could eat cakes and biscuits in bed that night. But Dame Twinkle's sharp eyes did see him. She pounced on him at once!

'Now, Frank, you take those things out of your pocket at once! None of your artful ways here! You're as sly as a fox, the way you behave!'

And a fox he was, a beautiful red fox, with a pointed nose, sharp ears and a wonderful tail. The children looked at him.

'Well, Frank always was a bit like a fox!' said Pam.

'He had such a sharp nose, hadn't he!'

'Really, this party seems to be turning into a zoo!' said Dame Twinkle, looking round at the birds and animals there. 'There are only a few of you left that are boys and girls. Well, well, well!'

She started them off on a hopping race round the garden, while she went to wash up the tea things. Hop-hop-hop they went down the path.

'Fanny's cheating!' cried Annie. 'She put her other foot to the ground.'

'You're cheating yourself!' cried John. 'Look at you – two feet on the ground now!'

'So are you, John!' said Benny, and he gave him a push. John pushed back. The other children hopped quickly ahead. The boys rushed after them to stop them.

'Begin again, begin again!' cried Annie. 'It's not fair! Benny, don't tug at my frock. You'll tear it.'

John told Benny off. 'You look as cross as a bear!' he said. And Benny became a bear – a nice, soft, fat little bear, with tears rolling down its nose because John had scolded it. He opened his big mouth to wail, but only a grunt came out.

Then the children began to quarrel again about who had won the hopping race. Annie knocked Elaine over. John pushed Annie. They screamed and behaved very badly indeed.

Dame Twinkle came running out, looking cross. Couldn't these children amuse themselves even for ten minutes without squealing and fighting?

'Now, now!' she cried. 'Stop fighting like cats and dogs! I'm ashamed of you!'

Well! All those who were squabbling at once became cats and dogs – and there they were, tails swinging or wagging, voices mewing or barking, a most astonished lot of creatures!

Dame Twinkle looked at them all.

'A goose – a donkey – a mouse – a peacock – a pig – a fox – a monkey – a bear – and any amount of cats and dogs!' she said. 'What a party! Well, I meant this to be a children's party, not a zoo meeting. You'd better all go home, and I'll save the supper lemonade and biscuits till tomorrow morning. Then, if you are nicely behaved boys and girls again, you can come and get them.'

So the donkey, the goose, the mouse, the peacock, the fox, the pig, the monkey, the bear and the cats and dogs all went rather sadly home, wondering what their mothers would say when they saw them.

But you will be glad to know that as soon as they reached their own gates they turned back into boys and girls again, much to their delight. So maybe they will get the lemonade and biscuits tomorrow after all.

What an astonishing party! Do you think you would have turned into a bird or animal if you had been there? And if so – what would you have been?

The Boy Who Was Too Clever

The Boy Who Was Too Clever

GEORGE WAS a very smart boy, and always at the top of his class for everything. He thought a lot of himself, and was sure no one was cleverer than he was.

One day he went walking on Breezy Hill, and there he found a small brownie in great trouble. The brownie had got his foot down a rabbit hole, and a naughty rabbit was holding on for all he was worth! Nothing the brownie said would make him leave go.

'Can you help me?' asked the brownie in despair, when he saw George coming along, and he told him what was happening.

'What will you give me if I help you?' asked George smartly.

'I'll give you a wish that will come true,' said the brownie.

'Good!' said George. 'Now I'll get you out of the fix you're in!'

He knelt down on the ground and began to make a noise like a fox. He barked sharply, just as a fox does in the night, and the rabbit below, holding on to the brownie's foot, heard the noise and was scared as could be! He let go of the brownie's foot at once and tore away down the burrow.

'Thank you,' said the brownie gratefully. 'Now, what is your wish?'

'I wish that all the wishes I ever wish will come true,' said George.

The brownie stared at him in surprise.

'You'll be sorry for that!' he said. 'You may think you're clever to think of wishing that *all* your wishes may come true, when I've only offered you one – but you'll find you are just too clever this time!'

'Oh, no, I shan't,' said George, very pleased with himself. The brownie ran off, and George went home, thinking of all the wishes he could wish!

Well, he had a grand time! He wished for chocolate ice cream bars, and he got them. He wished for treacle pudding at dinnertime, and he got it. He wished for a bag of toffees and a bag of chocolates, and there they were on the table beside him. Marvellous!

Then he began to feel ill because he had eaten such a lot, but he just wished he might be better, and he was! Aha! He could eat as much as he wanted, and never feel ill, because he had as many wishes as he liked. Clever George!

George had a lovely time that day. He wished for a pocketful of money, and he found shillings and sixpences and pennies jingling in his coat pocket. Then he thought he would go and buy what he liked out of the toy shop, but when he got there he thought it would be silly to spend his money, because he could easily wish for any of the things there and have them!

'I wish for that big ship!' he said, and lo and behold, it was in his hands! 'I wish for that football,' said George, and that came flying out of the shop too, and put itself into his arms! But then a policeman came by and thought that George must have stolen the things, and he ran after him!

But George didn't run for long. He just stood still and wished that the policeman would walk the other way, and he did!

Well, for some time things went very well for George, and then one day he was walking along the riverbank and he saw a little boy swimming in the water below. It was a hot day and George was puffing and blowing. He couldn't swim himself, and he was just a little bit afraid of the water. So he didn't wish to be out of his clothes and able to swim – no, he said something else!

He said, 'I wish I was that little boy and that little boy was me!'

And in a trice he found himself in the water, splashing about and swimming gaily. And on the bank stood someone looking like George, but who was really not George at all! How strange!

When George had had enough of swimming he thought he would change back to himself again, but no matter how much he wished, nothing happened! You see, he wasn't George now, he was the other little boy – and the other little boy's wishes never came true! So there was George properly caught, for nothing he could do could alter things. He had wished himself to be that boy, and that boy he was!

And what was more, that little boy was a poor little boy, with raggedy clothes, not enough to eat and hard work to do! So George found things were very different indeed, and many and many a time he wished he hadn't been quite so clever!

If I hadn't been so greedy over wishes I wouldn't be here now, he thought to himself, as he ran errands all day long. *I'd be George, a little boy with nice clothes, lots of toys and plenty of money!*

Sometimes he heard a little laugh, and he knew who it was – it was the brownie peeping round to see how George was getting on!

'I told you so!' the brownie said with a twittering laugh. 'I told you so!'

I wonder if George will change back to himself again! I expect he will one day!

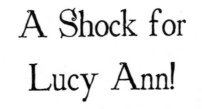

A Shock for
Lucy Ann!

A Shock for Lucy Ann!

LUCY ANN was a perfect nuisance. She was always putting her nose into other people's businesses, and interfering in other people's affairs.

'Oh, go away, Lucy Ann!' the children said, when she tried to show them how much better it would be to do things her way and not theirs. 'You are always interfering!'

'Oh, run away, Lucy Ann!' her mother would say, when Lucy Ann came poking round, telling her mother that this corner was not dusted, and that picture was hanging all crooked. 'I don't need you to come poking your nose everywhere! I can see dusty corners and crooked pictures for myself!'

'Oh, Lucy Ann, please go home!' said Mrs Brown, who lived down the road. 'I don't need *you* to tell me that my garden needs weeding, and that my roses need watering. You are always putting your nose into things that are no business of yours. Go away!'

Lucy Ann frowned and went away. But she didn't stop putting her nose into everything. She made herself such a nuisance that no one wanted her with them.

One day, as she was coming home over the fields, she heard voices talking, and she looked about to see where they came from. To her surprise she saw four little men sitting under the hedge, making daisy chains. But they were not making them in the way that Lucy Ann made them! Instead of threading the daisy heads through the stalks, they were tying the stalks together.

'Oh!' said Lucy Ann, poking her nose into their play at once. 'That's wrong! You shouldn't thread daisies that way! You want to do them like this!'

She snatched the daisies out of the hands of the surprised little men, and began to make holes through their stalks with a pin. The men jumped to their feet in anger – and then Lucy Ann saw that they were brownies. She stared at them, for she had never seen brownies before.

'You nasty, interfering little girl, poking your nose into our affairs!' cried one. 'Your nose wants seeing to – it's much too sharp!'

'Let's make it sharper still, so that when she goes about interfering and putting her nose where it isn't wanted, she'll always know!' cried the smallest brownie. He reached out his bony little hand and tapped Lucy Ann sharply on the nose.

'When you poke yourself here,
And poke yourself there,
Just grow longer and sharper
And make people stare,'

249

cried the brownie at the top of his voice.

'Oh!' cried Lucy Ann in a rage, for the tap hurt her. She was just going to push the brownie back when there came a puff of smoke from somewhere that hid the four little men – and when the smoke cleared away, the brownies had vanished.

Lucy Ann went home, very angry. Silly little men! She had only tried to show them the right way to make a daisy chain.

Just as she was nearly home she saw two boys she knew, playing marbles on the pavement. She stopped to watch.

'Oh, you silly!' she said to one. 'You will never win if you play like that. This is what you should do!'

As she was speaking a curious thing happened. Her nose grew very long indeed and very sharp. It poked itself among the marbles.

'Look! Look!' screamed the two boys in fright. 'Look at Lucy Ann's nose! It's like an elephant's trunk!'

Lucy Ann shrieked too. It was dreadful to feel

her nose waving about like that! She ran home crying loudly. But by the time she was indoors her nose had gone back to its right size again, and her mother laughed at her when Lucy Ann told her what had happened.

But she didn't laugh when she saw it happen again! And it soon did. It was when Lucy Ann's mother was busy reading a letter. Lucy Ann came and peeped to see what was in the letter, for she simply couldn't keep out of anything!

'Who's it from?' she said – and, dear me, just as she said that her nose shot out again, long and sharp and waving, and patted itself on to the letter.

Lucy Ann's mother gave a shriek. 'Oh!' she cried. 'How dreadful you look, Lucy Ann! Whatever has happened to your nose?'

Lucy Ann began to cry again. She told her mother about the brownies, and her mother nodded and frowned.

'Yes, you offended the little folk,' she said, 'and

they punished you. Now your nose will always grow long and sharp whenever you poke it where it isn't wanted. Oh, Lucy Ann, what a dreadful, dreadful thing! You had better come with me to old Mother Eleanor's. She knows a bit about magic and may put it right for you.'

So, crying bitterly, Lucy Ann went to Mother Eleanor's with her mother. But when Mother Eleanor heard what had happened, she laughed.

'I *could* take the spell out of her nose in a jiffy!' she said. 'But I shan't!'

'Oh, but what will poor Lucy Ann do!' cried her mother.

'Do?' said Mother Eleanor. 'Why, keep it right herself, of course! It only grows long and sharp when she pokes it where it isn't wanted, doesn't it? Well, if she stops poking her nose into everything it won't grow long and wave about like that!'

Lucy Ann went home with her mother, and thought hard. Her nose would never be cured – unless she cured it herself! She had better try. She wouldn't interfere with anyone. She would be sensible and say nothing, even when she badly wanted to poke her nose in somewhere!

Poor Lucy Ann! It wasn't so easy as she thought! Every day her nose shot out long and sharp, and every day people screamed at her or laughed loudly. But at last she tried so hard that a whole week went by and her nose stayed its right size and shape. And then she forgot again and out it shot, long and sharp, sticking itself here and there!

Lucy Ann was ashamed. She tried hard again – and, do you know, she hasn't let her nose grow long for more than a year now! She has gone to a new school, where the children don't know anything about the spell in her nose. I do hope she doesn't poke it where it isn't wanted again – because those children *will* be surprised to see what happens, won't they?

He Was Afraid!

ALAN HAD a new jacket. He was pleased with it because his old one had been much too short for him, and one of its sleeves had a patch over the elbow.

'Now you really look very nice in this new jacket,' his mother said to him. 'I feel proud of you in it! You look quite grown up. You will remember not to wear it except for going to school or going out to tea, won't you? You mustn't wear it when you go out to play, or else it will get dirty and torn.'

'I promise!' said Alan, and put his hands into the pockets to feel how nice and deep they were. He wished it was time to go to school. Then the others would see he had as good a jacket as theirs. They had so often teased him about his old, short one.

He kept his new one very nicely. He always hung it up on its peg at school. He hung it up as soon as he got home too, instead of flinging it down anywhere. His mother was pleased with him.

'You're really growing up, when you begin to take care of things,' she told Alan. 'That jacket is as nice now, after you've had it a month, as it was when I first tried it on you. Daddy's pleased about it too. He says if you're really learning to take care of your things he might give you a bicycle for your birthday, after all. He's always said no till now, because he was sure you wouldn't take care of it.'

'Oh, I'd love a bicycle!' said Alan, his face one big smile. 'Oh, Mother, do, do let me have one.'

Now, a week after this, Alan's friend, Peter, asked him to go and play with him on a Saturday morning. 'Take the short cut across the field,' he said. 'You get to our farm quicker that way.'

So, when Saturday morning came, Alan went to get his cap and jacket and scarf. He thought he had better put on his wellingtons too, because it had been raining hard and everywhere was muddy.

He looked into the cupboard where the jackets were kept. There were his two, the new one and the old one. He put his hand to take down his old one.

Then he frowned. 'No, I can't wear that. It's shorter than ever now I've grown a bit. It's all right to play in at home in the garden, but I really can't go to Peter's in it. Peter's mother would think I looked dreadful.'

Alan's mother was out shopping. Then she was going to see Granny. She wouldn't be back till Alan was home again from Peter's. So she wouldn't know which jacket he put on.

Alan pulled down his new jacket and put it on quickly. Then on went his scarf, cap and wellingtons, and he was ready.

Out he went, and ran all the way to Peter's. Peter was waiting for him. 'Hallo! My mother says it's too muddy to play out of doors, so let's go in and get out my trains,' he said.

Peter's mother was out, so Alan needn't have worried about which jacket to put on, after all! He hung his jacket up in the hall, and went to play with Peter. 'I've got to leave at twelve o'clock,' he said. 'Don't let me forget!'

'Right. And when you go, take the path up by the pigsties,' said Peter. 'There are some tiny piglets there, the funniest little things you ever saw.'

So, when Alan said goodbye, he took the path up to the pigsties. In one of them were eight little piglets, running about making funny noises. Alan thought they were very comical indeed. He climbed over the gate and went into the sty to play with the piglets.

But something suddenly got up out of the mud and charged at him with a fearful grunt! It was the old mother sow. She had been lying down quietly at the far end, and Alan hadn't noticed her because she was so dirty with mud.

Alan turned to run to the gate, but the sow ran right into him before he got there. He fell on his face in the mud. Two of the piglets ran over him in delight. The sow nosed him, and grunted loudly.

Alan got up, and the sow immediately knocked him over again. This time he rolled on his back. He shouted tearfully at the great animal, 'Go away! I wasn't doing any harm. Stop running at me!'

The sow waited till he had got up once more and then ran at him again. But this time Alan managed to get to the gate before he was knocked over. He scrambled over and caught his jacket on a nail. There was a tearing sound – and when he looked down, he saw a large hole in it.

Soon he was running home, trying not to cry. He looked at his jacket. It was covered with mud, and torn down the front. And it was his new jacket!

Alan stopped running. He felt frightened. What would his mother say? She had told him not to wear his new jacket when he went out to play. Now look at it! She would be so angry that she would tell his father, and he certainly wouldn't get him a bicycle for his birthday.

Alan's heart sank down and down. He hated being scolded. He hated being punished. He was afraid to tell his mother what had happened. *What shall I do?* he thought. *I daren't show Mother my jacket all torn and muddy like this! I daren't!*

He slipped in at the garden gate and tiptoed into the house. His mother wasn't back from seeing Granny. Annie, the cook, was busy getting dinner, and he could hear her in the kitchen. It was then that the Very Bad Idea came into his mind.

He tiptoed upstairs. He went to his cupboard and took down his old jacket. He took off his muddy new one and put on the old one. Then he tiptoed downstairs with the muddy new one and went out into the garden. He crumpled up the jacket as small as he could, and flung it over the wall at the bottom of the garden into some thick bushes that grew in the field beyond.

He felt frightened when he had done that, but he felt glad too. Now nobody would know his new jacket had been spoilt! He wouldn't be scolded. He would get a bicycle for his birthday. He had done a dreadful thing, he knew that, and he knew he was a coward because he had thrown away his jacket instead of being brave enough to own up that he had spoilt it.

'I don't care!' he kept saying to himself. 'I don't care! That sow shouldn't have knocked me over. It's her fault.'

It wasn't, of course. He knew perfectly well that he should have put on his old jacket to go and play with Peter. But he was afraid to think that. So he just kept on saying, 'I don't care! I don't care!'

Now, the next thing was, how was he to explain the disappearance of his new jacket? He walked into the house, thinking hard. Oh, dear, that would mean making up a story. Alan didn't much like that. He was a truthful boy in the ordinary way. He began to worry about what to say. Oh, what a muddle he was in – one horrid thing always seemed to lead to another!

But things were made unexpectedly easy for him. His mother came in at the front door as he came in at the garden door. 'Hallo, Alan!' she called. 'So you are just back from Peter's. I'm so glad you put on that old jacket. I forgot to remind you to be sure and wear that to go out to play.'

Alan didn't say a word. His mother came upstairs with him, and stood talking while he pulled off his outdoor things. She opened the cupboard door for him to hang up his jacket – and she suddenly saw the new coat wasn't there!

'Good gracious!' she said. 'Where's your new jacket? It was there this morning. I saw it. And you've been out all morning at Peter's wearing your *old* one! So somebody must have taken it while you were out. Oh, dear, what can have happened to it?'

She ran to the top of the stairs and called down, 'Annie! Has anyone been in the house this morning?'

'No, nobody!' called back Annie. 'Well, the window

cleaner came – but he only did the outside of the windows. He didn't come in.'

'The window cleaner!' said Mother. 'He must have slipped in at your window, Alan, and opened the cupboard door, seen your new jacket and taken it! I *know* it was there this morning, because I took a dirty hanky out of one of the pockets.'

Alan was really scared when he heard all this. His mother saw his frightened face. 'Now, don't you worry about it,' she said. 'I'll get it back for you. Don't look so scared. The man might have taken more valuable things than that.'

'But, Mother,' began Alan desperately. She didn't hear. She had gone into her own room and was busy looking round to make sure that nothing had been taken from there.

All sorts of things began to happen that weekend. That afternoon a workman walked through the field at the bottom of Alan's garden and caught sight of the crumpled-up mass of cloth in a bush there. He stopped to see what it was.

Maybe some old coat thrown away by a tramp, he thought, and pulled Alan's jacket out of the bush. He shook it out. It didn't look nice at all, and certainly no one would have thought it was new.

Dirty and torn – but my missis might clean it up for our young George, thought the workman, and rolled it up under his arm. *I suppose somebody's thrown it away – but what a place to throw it. Littering up the field like that! Still, maybe it will do for young George.*

When the mud had dried, George's mother took a brush and brushed the jacket hard. The mud brushed away easily. Then she mended the big tear very neatly indeed, so that it couldn't be seen at all. She called young George to her. He was a bit smaller than Alan, but the jacket looked very nice on him.

'Look at that!' said George's mother to her husband. 'I've made a new jacket of it! Plenty of wear in that, you know. What a shame to throw away a jacket as good as that is, just because it was dirty and torn.

Well, our George can wear it to school on Monday.'

So he did – and it so happened that Alan's mother was going shopping early, just as young George went to school. And she saw the jacket, of course!

She stopped at once and stared as if she couldn't believe her eyes. What! A strange little boy wearing Alan's new jacket. How had he got it?

She went up to George. 'Where did you get that jacket?' she asked. George looked astonished.

'My father found it,' he said.

Alan's mother didn't believe that for one moment.

'Is your father a window cleaner?' she asked.

'No. He's a bricklayer,' said George. 'My uncle's a window cleaner.'

Oho! thought Alan's mother. *Now I see what happened. The window cleaner took the jacket, and gave it to his brother. And now here's this boy wearing it – the window cleaner's nephew!*

She spoke again to George, who by now was feeling scared. 'Where do you live and what is your name?'

'I'm George White and I live in Rose Cottage, up on the hill,' said George. Then Alan's mother said no more, but walked on quickly.

She went straight to the police station! She was absolutely certain that George was wearing Alan's jacket which had been stolen by the window cleaner and passed on to George's father. Well, well, well!

'We'll look into the matter at once, madam,' said the policeman at the station. 'This man, the window cleaner, is known as a hard-working and respectable man. It's strange that he should suddenly steal a jacket.'

Alan had gone to school that morning in his old jacket. He had stayed to dinner, and he didn't get home till teatime. He had worried all day long about his spoilt new jacket and wished he hadn't thrown it away. He worried too because his mother had said it might have been stolen by the window cleaner, and he knew quite well it hadn't.

His mother gave him a terrible shock at teatime.

'Well, Alan, I've found your jacket!' she said. 'I was out shopping, and I suddenly saw young George White wearing it! He's the nephew of that window cleaner. He told some silly story about his father finding the jacket – finding it indeed! I am sure that it was his uncle who stole it when he came to clean the windows on Saturday, and passed it on to George's family.'

Alan went white. He couldn't think of a word to say. His mother went on talking. 'So I went to the police station and reported the matter. We shall soon get your jacket back now!'

Alan's father was having tea with them. He suddenly noticed Alan's white frightened face. 'What's the matter, Alan?' he said. But before Alan could answer there came a knock at the front door, and Annie came to say that the police sergeant wanted a word with Alan's mother. 'Show him in here,' said Alan's father, and in came the big sergeant. Alan began to shake at the knees.

'Good evening, madam, good evening, sir,' said the sergeant. 'About this jacket. Young George's father sticks to it that he found it in the middle of a bush in the field at the bottom of your garden. The window cleaner says he knows nothing about the jacket at all.'

'But how *could* the jacket have got into the middle of a bush in the field at the bottom of our garden?' began Alan's mother scornfully. Then her husband stopped her.

'Wait,' he said. 'It could have got there quite easily. Alan – what do you think about it?'

Alan was shaking. 'I f-f-feel sick,' he said.

'Well, go on feeling sick,' said his father sternly. 'But answer my question. DO YOU HEAR ME?'

There was a dead silence. The police sergeant waited, a notebook in his hand. Alan's mother held her breath. His father looked like a thundercloud.

Alan spoke at last, in a feeble cracking voice that didn't seem a bit like his own. 'I threw the jacket there. I got it muddy and torn, and I was afraid of what Mother would say. And I thought you wouldn't give me a bicycle if you knew I'd spoilt my coat.'

There was another silence. Then Alan's mother gave a sob. Alan's father turned to the sergeant. 'I'm sorry, Sergeant. Tell young George he can keep the coat. And give this five pound note to the window cleaner, with my sincere apologies for the mistake. I'll deal with Alan myself.'

Alan wondered if his father was going to send him to bed early. But he wasn't. He looked sternly and sadly at the frightened boy.

'Don't worry. I'm not going to punish you. See what an enormous punishment to have brought on yourself! You have lost your new jacket. You have lost your bicycle, because that money I gave the sergeant was saved up towards buying it. And you have lost the pride and trust that your mother and I have always had in you. If only you had been brave enough to come and own up that you'd dirtied and torn your jacket, none of this would have happened. You were afraid of a little scolding – and now you have to bear a very big punishment.'

Alan's mother put her arms round Alan. 'Oh, Alan! I do still trust you! You're not really a coward. You didn't know what awful things happen sometimes when you let yourself be afraid.'

'No, I didn't,' said poor Alan. 'But I know now. It shan't happen again, Mother. Please go on trusting me, please do. I don't mind so much about losing my jacket or my bike – but I do mind dreadfully if you don't trust me any more.'

'That's the way to look at it,' said his father, looking much less cross. 'I'll be proud of you yet!'

Well, I think he's right. Alan was afraid once – but he never will be again.

Mummy's New
Scissors

Mummy's New Scissors

MOTHER CAME into the playroom looking rather cross.

'My scissors are no longer in my workbasket,' she said. 'One of you children must have borrowed them – and they are my new scissors too. Who has taken them?'

'I haven't,' said Jean at once. 'I always ask you first.'

'What about you, Katie?' said her mother.

'Yes – oh, dear, I did borrow them,' said Katie. 'I couldn't ask you because you were out. I took them yesterday.'

'Why didn't you put them back?' said Mummy.

'The least anyone can do when they borrow anything is to put it back! Where are they?'

'I don't know,' said Katie, trying to remember. 'Let me see – I took them out into the garden to cut flowers.'

'Well, you must have brought them back,' said Mother. 'Where are they, Katie?'

'I'll go and look around the garden,' said Katie. 'I must have left them there.'

She ran out, ashamed, because she hadn't been careful with Mummy's bright new scissors. Thank goodness it hadn't rained in the night or they would be turning rusty.

She hunted everywhere for them, but she couldn't find them. She went back to tell her mother.

Mother frowned. 'You are always doing things like this, Katie. I can't have you growing up careless and forgetful. You will have to be punished. Those were my best new scissors – now I forbid you to play with your best new doll until you find my scissors.'

Katie didn't say anything, but she felt sad. She knew it was quite fair – but her best new doll was so lovely, and Katie took her out every single day for a walk.

Now I shan't be able to, she thought. *Poor Rosebud – she will wonder why. And I mustn't even play with her either.*

Jean ran up to her. 'Katie, you can't play with Rosebud, so may I? Do say I can. You've only let me hold her once, and I do love her. She's so pretty.'

'No, you can't,' said Katie at once. 'She's my doll. I won't let you play with her, if I can't.'

'All right,' said Jean, turning away. 'But I would be very, very careful – and I'm sure Rosebud will be unhappy with nobody at all to play with her and take her out. You're not very kind.'

Katie looked at Rosebud, lying peacefully in her cot. Rosebud looked back, and Katie thought she seemed puzzled. Was she wondering why Katie didn't pick her up and love her as she usually did?

'It isn't your fault I can't take you out and play with you,' said Katie suddenly. 'I am unkind. Jean's right. Jean! JEAN! Come back.'

Jean came back. 'You can play with Rosebud and take her out into the garden for a walk,' said Katie. 'I *will* let you, Jean.'

'Oh, thank you!' said Jean, pleased, and she ran to get Rosebud. She put on her pretty little rosebud hat and her new coat. How sweet she looked!

Then she carried her out into the garden. It was very windy indeed. Jean had to smooth Rosebud's clothes down, because they kept blowing up. And then her hat blew off!

'Oh, bother!' said Jean. 'Katie wouldn't like that at all. Sit still on this seat, Rosebud dear, while I get your hat.'

She sat Rosebud down carefully. Then she looked around for the hat. Where was it? She hunted here and she hunted there. Where could that little rosebud hat have gone?

Then she suddenly saw it. It was perched on top of a big spray of Michaelmas daisies and looked very strange indeed!

Jean ran to get it. The wind blew it off the daisies as she reached it, and it dropped down to the roots. Jean knelt down and put her hand among the stems to get it. She lifted up the hat – and caught sight of something shining underneath.

'Why!' she cried. 'It's Mummy's scissors! Katie! Quick, do come! See what I've found!'

She picked up the shining scissors and went to find Katie. She didn't run because her mother had said so often that it was dangerous to run with scissors – you might run into someone and hurt them with the scissor points.

She found Katie and handed her the scissors. 'Your doll's hat blew off into the Michaelmas daisies,' she said, 'and it dropped down to the ground and fell just on top of Mummy's scissors. Here they are!'

'Oh!' said Katie in delight. 'Thank you, Jean.

Mummy will be pleased. Now I can play with Rosebud again.'

'Oh, dear, so you can,' said Jean. 'I didn't have very long with her after all.'

'You shall have her as long as ever you like!' said Katie, and she hugged Jean. 'All the morning – and the afternoon too, if you want to. How clever of Rosebud's hat to find the scissors for me!'

She gave Mother back her scissors and told her how Rosebud's hat had found them. Mother laughed.

'It was really you who helped them to be found, Katie,' she said. 'You had the choice of being kind or unkind to Jean – but you chose to be kind and let her play with Rosebud, and so she was able to find the scissors. That's the way things work in this world, you know!'

Her mother was right, of course. It's the way things work – but it was funny that Rosebud's hat had to find the scissors, wasn't it?

The Very Funny
Tail

The Very Funny Tail

'BOTHER! HERE come those two bad children again!' said Tailer, the black cat. 'Run away, everyone!'

But Paddy-Paws was asleep on the wall, his long grey tail hanging down, and he didn't hear what Tailer said. The two children came nearer and saw him.

'Look!' said Katie. 'There's a fine tail to pull! Quick, pull it!'

Derek crept up to the sleeping cat. He caught hold of the hanging tail and pulled it hard.

'Wow!' yelled the cat, and leapt off the wall at once, angry and frightened.

'That's three tails we've pulled today,' said Katie.

'Look out for the next!'

That's what these two bad children loved to do –
pull tails. They even pulled cows' tails in the field,
and they would have pulled dogs' tails too, if they
had dared to.

All the cats were getting very tired indeed of
Katie and Derek. Things got worse instead of better,
for the two children really became very good indeed at
tugging all the tails they saw.

Now one day a new cat came to live nearby. He was
a Manx cat, and he had just a stump of a tail – for
Manx cats, as you know, never wear long tails.

The other cats came and looked at him. 'You are
very lucky,' said Tailer.

'Why?' asked Mankie in surprise.

'Because you've no long tail for Katie and Derek to
pull,' said Tailer, and he told Mankie all about the
two tiresome children.

Then Paddy-Paws had a marvellous idea. 'I say!'
he cried. 'Couldn't we play a trick on Katie and Derek?

They don't know Mankie, the cat without a tail, yet. Well, can't we get a tail from somewhere and tie it loosely on Mankie, and let him sit here on the wall with it hanging down? Then, when the two children come along and pull it, it will come off and give them such a shock they will never, never pull our tails again!'

'That's really a very bright idea,' said Tailer, and Sooty, Fluff and Tabby nodded their furry heads.

'The thing is – what about a tail?' wondered Paddy-Paws. 'Where could we get that from?'

'I know!' cried Fluff, who belonged to the children's own mother. 'I know! My mistress has an old fur with a tail to it. I could bite off that tail and we could tie it to Mankie!'

'Good idea!' said Tailer. 'Go and get the tail.'

Fluff raced off. She made her way to her mistress's bedroom, and found the fur hanging in a cupboard. With her sharp teeth she nibbled and gnawed at that fur until the tail dropped off on to the floor beside Fluff.

Fluff gave a giggle. The tail looked funny all by itself. It was long and thick and silvery black. She picked it up in her mouth, and without anyone seeing her she ran down the stairs with it and out into the garden.

'Oh, good!' said the waiting cats. 'What a fine tail! Now we'll tie it on to Mankie.' But they couldn't seem to tie it very well because their claws kept getting in the way, so they asked the little grey squirrel to help. He was used to using his paws and he tied the tail on quite easily.

'Now sit on the wall, Mankie, and hang the tail down,' cried Tailer in delight. So Mankie sat on the wall and hung the new tail down. Really, he looked rather odd, for he was a small cat, and the tail was very big and thick. Still, it looked exactly as if it belonged to him, so that was all right.

Well, soon the two children came that way home from their walk. They at once saw Mankie on the wall and they nudged one another. 'Look! There's a beautiful tail to pull!' said Katie. 'Whose turn is it to pull one?'

'Mine,' said Derek, and he crept towards Mankie, who carefully looked the other way.

Derek put out his hand. He got hold of the tail. He gave it an enormous pull – and oh, my goodness gracious me, it came right off in his hand!

'Oh!' cried Derek, really frightened. 'Katie! Katie! I've pulled the tail right off!'

Katie looked at the cat. Sure enough it now only had a little stump of a tail. She gave a squeal of fright and began to cry. 'It's got no tail now! You've pulled it off! Oh, you wicked boy!'

'Well you'd have pulled it off if it had been your turn,' said Derek, half crying too.

'No, I shouldn't. I wouldn't have pulled so hard!' cried Katie. 'Oh, the poor cat! What will its people say when it goes home without a tail?'

The two tiresome children were really very much upset and afraid. It was one thing to pull a tail for a joke, but quite another to pull one right off. They were so frightened that they ran to their mother, sobbing.

'What's the matter?' asked Mother at once.

'Mummy, we've pulled a cat's tail right off!' sobbed Katie.

'What? Right off?' said Mother, alarmed. 'You bad, bad children! How many times have I told you not to pull tails? Now you will get into serious trouble with the cat's owner.'

The children sobbed and cried, and their mother sent them to fetch the cat's tail from the lane outside, where they had left it. They picked it up and brought it to her.

'This is a strange tail for a cat to have,' said Mother in surprise. 'It is more like a fox's tail – a silver fox's, I should think.'

'No, Mummy, it grew on the cat that sat on the wall,' said Katie. 'It did really.'

'Well, I'll show you how like a fox's tail it is,' said

Mother. 'Come upstairs and I'll show you my silver fox fur, which used to belong to Granny, and you will see how alike the two tails are.'

So they all went upstairs, and Mother took the fur from the cupboard. But suddenly she saw that the tail was missing!

'The tail is gone!' she cried. 'This is the tail! You cut the tail off Granny's fur, you naughty, bad children!'

'Mummy, we didn't!' cried Derek. 'It came off the cat.'

'I don't believe you,' said Mother. 'I am quite, quite sure that this tail belongs to Granny's fur. I think you have made up this story of the cat because you knew you would get into trouble if you owned up that you had taken the fur's tail.'

And do you know, nothing that Katie or Derek said would make their mother believe that they had not taken the tail. She sent them both to bed early. When Fluff heard this she flew out to tell all the other cats.

'You can't imagine how well the trick worked!' she cried. 'It was simply marvellous! I don't think those children will ever pull our tails again.'

Fluff was right – and dear me, when poor Katie and Derek catch sight of Mankie, the cat without a tail, they feel quite ill and look the other way. Nobody has told them yet that Mankie never had a tail, so they still think they pulled it off! Didn't they get a shock?

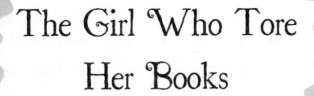

The Girl Who Tore
Her Books

The Girl Who Tore Her Books

ANNA WAS a funny little girl. She took great care of her toys, especially her dolls – but, dear me, how naughty she was with her books!

She liked nothing better than to tear the pages into small bits! As soon as she was left alone in the nursery she would take a book from the shelf, sit down on the floor with it and then find a picture. In two seconds the picture was torn in half! Her mother gave her old newspapers to tear up, but Anna didn't want those. It was books she loved to tear.

And then one day something happened. She was alone in the nursery after tea. There was no light except the firelight that flickered everywhere. Anna crept to the shelf and took down a big nursery rhyme book that her mother had forbidden her to touch.

She badly wanted to tear up the pictures of the nursery rhyme folk inside, and throw the pieces over the floor. She opened the book at the page where the Old Woman looked out of her shoe. And just as she was going to tear the shoe in half, a strange feeling came over her.

She felt giddy and shut her eyes. She opened them and looked at her book – but what was happening? The shoe seemed to be growing right out of the book – it was getting bigger and bigger and bigger! The Old Woman was getting bigger too – her mouth was opening and shutting, and Anna could hear her talking!

'Come to bed, children!' she was saying. 'Come to bed! I've got your broth ready for you!'

The shoe became so big that it almost filled the nursery! Then Anna saw crowds of small children running round it, shouting and laughing. The Old Woman clapped her hands and cried loudly, 'Come along, come along!'

Three of the children ran up to Anna, and looked at her.

'What a funny little girl!' they said. 'She doesn't look real! She's made of paper!'

Anna looked down at herself in surprise. She *did* look rather queer! She had gone very, very thin, almost as thin as paper. How strange! She looked as if she had been cut out of a picture book.

'Mother! Mother! Come and look at this funny little girl!' cried the children. 'Is she a paper girl?'

The Old Woman stepped out of her shoe house and walked over to where Anna stood. She looked at her in surprise.

'Why, it's the naughty little girl I have so often heard about!' she said. 'She is the one who tears all her nice picture books to pieces. Something magic has happened. She is made of paper herself now.'

'Oh, Mother, do let's tear her then!' cried the children, dancing round. 'It won't hurt her if she's made of paper.'

'It *will* hurt me,' said Anna, crying in fright. 'I know it will. Don't touch me.'

'Oh, do let's try and see!' said a small boy, taking hold of Anna's arm. 'Just let me tear a bit of your arm. You are always tearing up people in books. Now it is your turn.'

Anna jerked away her arm. 'Don't!' she said. 'If you try to tear me, I'll shout for my mother.'

'She isn't here,' said a little girl. 'There's only our mother here, and she will put you to bed if you make too much noise.'

'Well, I won't be torn up,' said Anna. 'I am not made of paper, though I may look as if I am. I shall go back to my own proper self in a minute, I expect, and if you tear me now I might find myself without an arm or something later on. Leave me alone.'

'But you always tear up your books,' said the little

boy, dancing round Anna. 'If you tear paper people, why can't we?'

'I wish I hadn't now,' said poor Anna. 'I'll never do it again!'

A big boy went behind Anna and took hold of her paper dress. There was a sound of tearing, and Anna screamed in fright.

'You've torn my dress! Oh, you've torn my dress! You bad, naughty boy!'

'It's only paper,' grinned the boy. 'Ha, ha! Now I've torn your dress just as you've often torn the dresses of people in books! How do you like it?'

Anna flew at the big boy. He yelled out, and all the other children shouted. The Old Woman came out from her shoe again with a frown on her face. She caught hold of one child after another and pushed them into the shoe.

'You'll get some broth without any bread, and then you'll be sent to bed!' she grumbled. 'Fighting like that! I'm ashamed of you!'

She caught hold of Anna too, but the little girl, afraid of being made one of the shoe children, wriggled away. The Old Woman caught hold of her dress – and it tore once again!

Anna was pushed into the shoe with all the other children. She looked about for a way to escape, but the Old Woman shut the shoe door tightly and locked it. Anna saw another door at the back and ran for it.

'Come back, you naughty girl!' cried the Old Woman – but Anna had opened the door and was running out as fast as she could!

There were some stairs in front of her and she ran down them panting. At the bottom she bumped into someone, and a voice said, 'Anna dear! Whatever is the matter?'

It was her mother, just coming up the stairs! Anna stopped and looked round. She was at the bottom of the stairs that led to the nursery! How very strange! She looked down at herself, but it was dark, and she couldn't see if she was still made of paper.

'Mother! Feel me! Am I made of paper or am I real again?' cried Anna, holding on to her surprised mother.

'Anna, you must have been dreaming,' said her mother, taking her upstairs to the nursery and switching on the light. 'Of course you're not made of paper, darling!'

Anna looked down at herself, and sighed with relief. Yes, she was her old solid, real self again.

Then her mother frowned. 'Oh, Anna, look how you've torn your frock! In two places! However did you do that?'

'Mother, a boy from the shoe tore it, and so did the Old Woman when I ran away,' said Anna.

But of course her mother didn't believe her, and she scolded Anna hard.

'It is very, very naughty of you to spoil that nice frock,' she said. 'You are always tearing books – and if you start tearing frocks too, I shall have to send you to bed each time you do it. I am very angry, Anna.'

Anna began to cry. 'I am not going to tear my books

any more,' she said. 'Please believe me, Mother. I promise I won't.'

Well, she didn't. She had to mend her torn frock herself, and it took her one whole morning. And now, when her mother wants to read her nursery rhymes, Anna always turns over the page about the Old Woman and won't let it be read. I am not surprised, are you?

The Naughty
Little Storyteller

The Naughty Little Storyteller

THERE WAS once a boy called Benjy who was a naughty little storyteller. He just didn't bother to tell the truth when he was asked.

If his mother said to him, 'Benjy, is it six o'clock yet, your bedtime?' he would say, 'No, Mother, it's only ten to.'

And then the clock would strike six, so his mother knew he was telling stories! She didn't know what to do with him, and neither did his teacher.

But someone else knew what to do. Just listen!

As Benjy was coming home from school one day, he met an old woman. She said to Benjy, 'Good morning, little boy. Are you going to the village? If you are, take me with you, because I don't know the way.'

Now Benjy *was* going to the village, for that was where he lived – but he wasn't going to say so, because he wanted to run home and not walk slowly with an old woman. So he said, 'No, I'm not going to the village, I'm afraid. But you'll easily find it. It's across this field, and over the stile and down the road, and—'

'You are a naughty little storyteller, Benjy,' said the old woman suddenly, looking at him with wide-open, piercing eyes. 'You *are* going to the village! Well, you won't go there this morning, anyhow! Come with me!'

She took hold of his arm and Benjy had to go with her. He was rather frightened. The old woman led him through a hole in the hedge that he had never noticed before, and into a lane that was quite new to him. Down the lane they went to a village that Benjy was most surprised to see – for in it were brownies, gnomes, pixies, witches and even a big giant, who, however, was full of smiles and not at all frightening.

'You might let me go,' said Benjy, pulling at the old woman's arm. 'My mother has a chocolate pudding for my dinner today, and I'm hungry. She will be cross with me if I'm late.'

'Very well then, go!' said the old dame, and she let go of Benjy's hand. He darted away up the lane down which they had come – but somehow it seemed different – and to his surprise he came, before long, to a tumbledown cottage, outside which sat a long-nosed brownie, knitting a red sock.

'Please,' said Benjy, 'could you tell me the way home? I want to get to Hillside Village.'

'Yes, certainly,' said the brownie, beaming. He pointed across a field with his knitting needle. 'Just trot across that field and you're there!'

So away trotted Benjy across the field – but, dear me, on the other side of the field was a broad river and he couldn't possibly get across. He frowned angrily at the water.

'That horrid brownie told me an untruth!' he said. 'I know my home isn't this way.'

He saw a little man coming up the river path and he called him. 'I say! Which is the way to Hillside Village?'

'Catch the bus at the corner!' said the little man, pointing to where a lane turned a corner nearby. Benjy ran to the corner and stood there. He stood there for five minutes. He stood there for ten minutes. He stood there for *twenty* minutes! Still no bus. Then he saw a brownie boy and shouted to him, 'How soon does the bus come along?'

'What bus?' asked the boy in surprise.

'The bus that goes from here to Hillside Village, of course,' said Benjy.

'There isn't one,' said the boy, grinning. 'Someone's been telling you a story!'

Benjy was too angry to speak.

'If you want to get to Hillside Village, you must walk up the hill there, down the other side, across a field where you'll see some geese and then over the stile in the corner,' said the brownie boy. 'But it's no good waiting for a bus, because one won't come.'

'Thank you,' said Benjy, and walked off. He climbed the hill, which was very steep. He went down the other side. He came to the field and saw some geese there. He walked into the field – and all the geese chased him with hisses and cackles till he reached the stile in the corner – and there he found a red-faced farmer waiting for him!

'What are you doing in my field?' he roared.

'Nothing,' said poor Benjy. 'Only just trying to find my way home to Hillside Village.'

'Well, you won't find it *this* way,' said the farmer angrily. 'Disturbing all my geese! I've a good mind to punish you! You've come the wrong way for Hillside Village. You want to go right in the opposite direction. Someone's told you a story if they said come this way!'

'This is a hateful place for telling stories,' said Benjy almost in tears. 'Everyone tells me stories.'

'Dear me, that's strange,' said the farmer, looking closely at Benjy. 'I wonder why they do. Is it anything to do with yourself, do you think?'

'I don't know what you mean,' said Benjy, going red.

'Oh, well, think about it,' said the farmer, going off. 'I just wondered.'

Benjy sat on the stile and thought about it. Could it be that everyone was telling him stories because he himself was a storyteller? Had that old woman been punishing him like that – making everyone behave to him as he had behaved to everyone else? How perfectly horrid!

'I don't like it a bit,' said Benjy out loud. 'I've walked miles – all for nothing. I've stood ages waiting for a bus that didn't come. I'm hungry as can be, and I know Mother will be very cross. Perhaps she won't have saved me any chocolate pudding at all.'

'Hallo, Benjy,' said a voice. Benjy looked round. He saw the same old woman that he had seen at first. 'How do you like storytellers?'

'I don't like them at all,' said Benjy.

'Neither do I,' said the old woman. 'They are most unpleasant people, aren't they?'

'Yes,' said Benjy, 'and I'm going to stop being one now I know what they are like.'

'Good,' said the old woman. 'Well, you can go home now. Get over the stile and you'll know where you are.'

Benjy hopped over the stile – and to his great surprise he found that he was just at the end of his road. How strange! He rushed home at once. His mother met him at the door with a frown.

'You're very late, Benjy,' she said. 'What happened? I suppose you'll tell me some story or other, so I might just as well not ask you.'

'I'll tell you the *truth*,' said Benjy, and he told his mother everything that had happened. His mother was most astonished.

'Well,' she said, 'I'll believe all this if you *do* turn over a new leaf, Benjy, and never tell stories again!'

Benjy always does tell the truth now – but wasn't it queer how he learnt his lesson!

A Story of Tidiness and Untidiness

A Story of Tidiness
and Untidiness

THERE WERE once two little girls called Julie and Jean. They were twins and did everything together.

One day their little brother caught chickenpox, and Mother didn't want Julie and Jean to catch it too.

'I wonder who would have you to stay with them for a little while,' she said. 'You can't go to Aunt Kate's, she's away. I wonder if Great-Aunt Jane would have you?' Mother phoned to see. Great-Aunt Jane said she would have Julie and Jean, but they would have to make themselves useful around the house.

'Well, you two girls know how to dust and sweep

and make your own beds,' said Mother, 'so you must just offer to do that for Great-Aunt Jane.'

Off went Julie and Jean, rather excited to be going away to stay, and quite determined to do all they could to help their great-aunt.

Great-Aunt Jane lived in a dear little cottage, with a lovely garden full of flowers. She had two little puppies and a tiny kitten that played with them all day long. In the garden she had a little round pond with goldfish in it. Julie and Jean were very excited when they saw all these lovely things.

'Puppies and a kitten to play with!' said Julie.

'And a goldfish pond to sail boats on!' cried Jean. 'What fun we'll have.'

The next morning Great-Aunt Jane called them into her kitchen, where she was busy feeding the puppies and the kitten.

'I told Mother you would have to make yourselves useful around the house,' she said, looking at them over the top of her big spectacles. 'What can you be trusted to do? Girls don't work half as well nowadays as they used to in my young days.'

'Great-Aunt, we will work well!' said Jean. 'We can be trusted to do lots of things. We can dust and sweep and make our beds.'

'Very well. Make your beds each morning. And Julie, you can dust the dining room and sweep it and Jean can dust and sweep the sitting room. Keep your own room tidy too. I'll come and watch you this morning. You'll have to work hard, you see,' Great-Aunt Jane chuckled at the twins.

They laughed. 'Oh, that isn't much!' said Julie. 'We shall soon get that done! Then we'll be able to play in the garden with the puppies, won't we?'

'Yes, you may,' said Great-Aunt Jane. 'But you must do your jobs thoroughly, do you understand? A job which is only half done is a disgrace to any girl or boy!'

Then she took them upstairs and watched them while they made their beds and tidied their room.

Then downstairs they went and showed her how they dusted and swept.

'That's very nice, very nice indeed,' said Great-Aunt Jane. 'I hope you'll do it like that every morning.'

The twins ran out into the garden. 'Isn't Great-Aunt particular?' said Julie. 'It's an awful bother to dust in every corner like that.'

'Well, Mummy's particular too,' said Jean, who liked doing things well.

Julie didn't. She was an untidy little girl, and she usually left everything for Jean to do. But she couldn't at her great-aunt's because they each had different things to do.

The next day both little girls did their morning jobs. They straightened their sheets, plumped up the pillows and made their beds beautifully. And each of them dusted and swept as carefully as could be. Then out they went to play with the puppies and to watch the goldfish as it swam.

But the next morning, Julie couldn't be bothered to

dust properly. *What does it matter if I leave the dark corners undusted!* she thought. *Nobody will see if I don't do them! And I do so want to go out into the garden and see what it can be that those puppies are squealing about!*

So out she went long before Jean, who was giving the sitting room a very good dusting.

Next morning it was just the same. Julie didn't bother a bit about dusting in the corners. Nor did she on the next day, which was Saturday. She was out in the garden long before Jean.

But as Jean was dusting carefully behind a big saucer on the china cabinet, she came across a funny little flat parcel. She picked it up. On it was written:

For Jean, with Great-Aunt's love. Buy a boat with this to sail on the goldfish pond.

Jean opened it. Inside was some money!

'Oh, how lovely!' cried Jean, rushing to thank Great-Aunt Jane. 'What a good thing it was that I remembered to dust behind that saucer!'

She ran to show Julie. Julie was delighted to think they would have a boat to sail on the pond, but a little bit hurt because Great-Aunt Jane hadn't given her some money too. They bought a lovely boat and had a glorious time sailing it on the pond. Julie did so wish she had one as well.

The days went by and the little girls did their work every morning. Great-Aunt Jane never seemed to go and look how they were doing it, so Julie started to become more and more careless. She made her bed badly, and she didn't plump the pillows once. The next Saturday that came she bundled her bed together anyhow, and ran quickly downstairs to sail the boat before Jean came.

But Jean was a long time coming! She had made a lovely discovery. As she made her bed she saw something long and flat lying beneath the pillows. She picked it up and undid the paper. It was a book of fairy tales, with lots of pictures!

'How perfectly lovely!' cried Jean, and ran to thank Great-Aunt Jane again.

'I'm glad you like it,' said Great-Aunt, smiling at her. 'I know you must have made your bed properly, my dear, if you found that.'

When Jean showed the book to Julie, Julie began to cry. 'Nasty old Great-Aunt Jane, to give you things and not me!' she sobbed. 'Mummy always gives us the same. Why doesn't Great-Aunt Jane?'

Just at that moment Great-Aunt came out. 'Dear, dear, dear!' she said. 'What's all this to-do?'

'Julie's crying because you didn't give anything to her,' said Jean. 'Why didn't you, Great-Aunt?'

'Oh, but I did!' said Great-Aunt Jane. 'Come and see.'

She took the two little girls into the dining room that Julie was supposed to dust each morning.

'Did you dust behind the clock on the mantelpiece?' she asked Julie.

Julie went very red. She knew there were lots of

corners in the room she had missed. 'No,' she said, 'I didn't.'

'There now!' said Great-Aunt Jane. 'And I put some money for you there last Saturday, because I wanted to pay you for dusting so nicely. Well, well. I must have it back, as you didn't dust properly. See if it's there.'

Julie peeped behind the clock. Yes, there was a little flat parcel with *Julie* written on it. And wasn't it dusty!

Great-Aunt Jane solemnly undid the parcel and put the money back into her purse. Then she took them upstairs to their bedroom.

'Did you plump your pillows this morning?' she asked Julie.

Julie hung her head and said no, she hadn't.

'Dear, dear, dear!' said Great-Aunt Jane. 'Then I suppose your fairy tale book is still under the pillows! Why don't you take a look and see!'

It was! And very sadly Julie watched her great-aunt

put it away in a cupboard. She was terribly ashamed and made up her mind never ever to do her work carelessly again.

'You are going home today,' said Great-Aunt Jane, 'and you may each take a puppy for your own, because I have enjoyed having you. Jean, go on doing your jobs well, and you will be a great help to your mother. Julie, don't forget the lesson you have learnt while you have been here with me!'

And the funny old lady smiled at them so kindly that Julie smiled back through her tears and thought what a silly girl she had been.

Then the twins went upstairs, packed up all their things in their bags, tucked their puppies under their arms and went downstairs again to say goodbye to Great-Aunt Jane.

When Julie said goodbye to her great-aunt, she kissed her and whispered something into her ear. 'I'm sorry I worked so very badly,' she said, 'but I promise I never will again.'

Great-Aunt waved goodbye to them as they went off. The twins were sorry to leave the dear little cottage, but they were most excited to be going home to their parents again.

'Whatever do you think Mummy will say when she sees our puppies?' said Jean.

Mother was delighted to have her two little girls home again, and Great-Aunt Jane had already asked her if the twins might have the puppies. She wondered why Jean had a ship and a book as well, while Julie had none, but she asked no questions.

But she was surprised to find, after only a few days, that instead of one very tidy little girl and one very untidy little girl, she had two of the tidiest little daughters you can imagine.

She couldn't make it out. Julie's bed was always as well made as Jean's, and instead of hurry-scurrying over it and getting everything done first, she found that Julie was often longer than Jean.

'Well, really!' said Mother to Father one night.

'I honestly don't believe any mother has got two such thorough little girls as we have. I really don't think you'd be able to find a single speck of dust anywhere in the house, no matter how hard you looked!'

Julie and Jean were very pleased to hear that, and Julie was delighted when Mother said she really must phone Great-Aunt Jane and tell her how helpful the twins were.

Two days afterwards there came a great rat-tat-tat at the door. Mother opened it, and took a big, exciting-looking parcel from the postman.

'Why, it's addressed to Julie!' she said.

Julie was most excited. She undid the string and opened the parcel.

Inside was a lovely fairy tale book! There was a letter too, and when Julie opened it, some money fell out!

Dear Julie, wrote Great-Aunt Jane.

I think these belong to you now, don't they? If you buy

a ship like Jean's, do please come and stay with me
again and sail it on my pond. Don't forget to come soon,
will you?

Wasn't that nice of Great-Aunt Jane?

The Enchanted Book

The Enchanted Book

THIS IS an odd story. It is about John, a boy who lived in London fifty years ago. John is grown up now, of course, and he doesn't know if it was all a dream or if it really happened. You must decide for yourself when you read the story.

John was eight years old. He was just an ordinary boy, going to school every day, working, playing, eating and going to bed at night, just as you do.

He was naughty sometimes, just as you are. He was kind sometimes, just as you are. When he was naughty his mother and teachers scolded him. When he was kind they loved him. Sometimes they said,

'You must be honest. You must be patient. You must be unselfish.'

But they didn't tell him exactly *why* he must. He thought about it a little, and then he said to himself, 'I don't see that it matters very much if I tell a little lie now and again. No one will know. And if I buy sweets and eat them all myself, why shouldn't I? No one will know. And what does it really matter that I took Harry's rubber the other day and didn't give it back? He didn't know I took it. As long as nobody knows, I can't see that it matters.'

And then one day something happened to him that showed him the real reason why all those things did matter.

At that time John was sort of half-and-half. That is, he sometimes told the truth, and he sometimes didn't. He was sometimes kind, and sometimes unkind. He was sometimes quite honest, and sometimes not. A lot of children are like that. John could be very mean and spiteful and rough – but he could also be very generous and unselfish and gentle. He was just about half-and-half. Half good and half bad.

Now one day, when he was still a half-and-half, he went shopping by himself. He went down an old, old street in London, peering into shops that sold old, old things. They were dusty, and they looked sad and forgotten. There were curious mirrors with dragons carved round the frames. There were old china ornaments – spotted dogs and funny cats, and some shepherdesses with sheep. There were old chairs, some of them so big that John half wondered if they had belonged to giant men.

He saw a dear little workbasket that had once belonged to an old lady many years ago. On the lid were two letters made of mother-of-pearl. They shone prettily. The letters were M.L. John stared at them, and a thought came into his head.

'M.L.,' he said to himself. 'Mother's name is Mary Lomond. What fun if I bought that basket for her birthday! I'll ask how much it is.'

He went into the shop. The funniest old man came out of the dark part of the shop – *rather like an old spider coming out of its web*, John thought.

'How much is this basket, please?' asked John.

'Ten shillings,' said the old man.

John stood and thought. He had almost ten shillings at home, but he had meant to buy himself a penknife with some of it. He badly wanted a penknife. All the boys in his class had a penknife except John. If he spent all his money on the basket, he wouldn't be able to have the penknife. So, after thinking for a while, John shook his head.

'I've only got about five shillings,' he said. This wasn't true, but he didn't want to explain to the man that he almost had enough but wanted to spend some on himself. The old man nodded.

'Look around and see if there's anything else,' he said. He hobbled off and left John in the untidy, musty, dusty old shop. The boy began to look around. He looked at a set of old games. He tried all the drawers in a funny old desk. He looked at some of the old books on a shelf.

And it was there he found what he always afterwards called the Enchanted Book. It was an enormous book, and the cover shone strangely, almost as if it was on fire. When he was looking at the cover the old shopman appeared again. 'You'd better not look at that book,' he said. 'That's a dangerous book. It's got *you* in it.'

John was startled. 'What do you mean?' he said.

'It's a strange book,' said the old man. 'Anyone who looks well into it will see himself in the future. I wouldn't look, if I were you. You might not like what you see.'

'Why not?' asked John puzzled. 'I'm going to be a doctor. I'd like to see what I look like as a grown-up doctor. I'm going to be a clever doctor. I'm not only going to make people well, I'm going to make a lot of money too.'

'I wouldn't look in that book if I were you,' said the

old man, and he tried to take the book away. 'Look here, my boy, I'm old and I know a lot. You've got a mouth that looks a bit hard to me. You've a wrinkle over your eyes that tells me you can be unkind. You've a look in your eyes that tells me you don't always speak the truth. Don't you look into that book. You'll see something that will make you afraid and unhappy.'

Well, that made John feel he simply must see the pages of that book. He couldn't really believe that they would show him himself, but he felt that he must find out.

'I want to see,' he said. 'Please, do let me see. I won't damage the book in any way.'

He looked up at the old man and smiled. Now John's smile was very nice. His eyes lit up, and creased at the corners, his mouth curved merrily and his whole face changed. The old man looked at him closely.

'I believe you're half-and-half,' he said. 'If you are, this book will show you two stories with pictures –

one story will begin at the beginning of the book. The other one you'll find by turning the book the other way and opening it at the end. If you're half-and-half – that is, half good and half bad – there's no harm in letting you see the book. All right. Have your own way. We'll open the book at this end first.'

The old man opened the book and John stared in great surprise for there was a picture of himself, in jersey and short trousers, just as he was then.

'You,' said the old man, and turned a page. 'Here you are doing something you're ashamed of – ah, yes – cheating at sums. Dear, dear, what a pity! And here you are boasting about something you hadn't really done. And look – what's this picture? You're bigger here – about two years older, I should think. You are telling an untruth without even going red! You're winning a prize, but only because you told that untruth.'

'I don't like this book,' said John, and he tried to close it. The old man stopped him.

'No. Once you've opened it, you've got to go on. Look at this picture – you're quite big here. You're being unkind to a smaller boy, but there's no one to see, so you don't mind. Nasty little bully! And oh, look here – who's this? Your mother?'

'Yes,' said John. 'Why is she crying in the picture?'

'Because she's so disappointed in you,' said the old man. 'Look, it's her birthday – she's got a birthday card in her hand. She wanted you to spend her birthday with her, and you had promised to but at the last moment somebody asked you to go to a picnic and you went there instead. You didn't really mind if your mother was sad or not. She's thinking about you – feeling disappointed that you are growing up into a selfish, boastful, unkind youth.'

'I don't like that picture,' said John in a trembling voice. 'Turn the page, quick.'

The page turned. 'Why, here you're grown up!' said the old man. 'Fine-looking fellow too. You're studying to be a doctor. You said you meant to be one, didn't you? Well, you are going to be. This man here in this picture with you is saying that to be a doctor is a wonderful thing – you can bring healing and happiness to people who need it. But you are laughing and saying, "That's all very well, I'll do that all right – but I'll be a rich man too. I'll make people pay all I can".'

John said nothing. He didn't like himself at all in the pictures. The old man turned to him. 'You mustn't be surprised at what you see,' he said gravely. 'After all, you tell stories now, you are sometimes hard and unkind, you are not always honest and I can see you are often selfish. Well, those things grow, my boy, they grow – and this is what they grow into!'

The pages turned again. John saw himself getting older and older. He saw himself getting rich. He saw himself with a pretty wife, with happy children. He saw himself getting older still, and his face was not pleasant. It was hard and selfish.

He saw himself being pleasant to rich people, and

rough with poor ones. He saw himself cheating when he could do it without being found out. He saw himself being bad-tempered at home, and unkind to the children. And then, alas, came some dreadful pictures, when he had been found out in some wrongdoing, and had lost all his money! His children left home when they were old enough because they hated him, and his pretty wife grew ugly and bad-tempered because she was lonely and unhappy.

'I hate this book!' cried John. The pictures had come to an end. The old man turned the book round the other way and opened the pages from the end instead of the beginning.

'Wait,' he said. 'I told you you were a half-and-half, didn't I? We'll see what the other half of you might lead to.'

And there, page by page, was the story of what would be John's life if the good half of him grew, instead of the bad.

You should have seen those pictures! He won

prizes, not by cheating, but by hard work. He gained friends, not by boasting, but by kindness. His mother smiled out from the story, happy in an unselfish and loving son. There he was, studying to be a doctor, but this time not boasting that he meant to be rich. This time he was saying something else, 'The world is divided into two kinds of people – the ones who help and the ones who have to be helped. I'm going to be one who helps. I don't care if I make money or not – but I do care if I make happiness.'

And there was his wife again, and his happy children. But this time they loved him, gave him a great welcome whenever he came home. They hadn't so much money – but how proud they were of John. How the sick people loved him, and how happy he was. His face was not so hard as in the other pictures. It was kind and happy. It was the face of a great and a good man.

'Well, there you are,' said the old man, shutting the book up softly. 'You're a half-and-half, as I said.

Let the bad half of you grow, and it will grow into a bad man. Let the good half grow, and you'll get plenty of happiness and give it to others as well. Ah, my boy, there's a reason for not telling fibs, for not being dishonest, for not being unkind, for not cheating, for not being mean. We've all got the choice when we're small of letting one half of ourselves grow or the other half. Nobody else but ourselves can choose.'

'Yes,' said John in a small voice.

'You may think to yourself, "Nobody knows I'm telling a fib",' said the old man. 'But *you* know it. That's what matters. It makes the wrong half grow, you see. Well, my boy, you'd better get back home now. And never mind about that workbasket. I can easily sell it to someone else if you haven't enough money.'

'I have enough money,' said John. 'At least, I shall have tomorrow, when Father gives me my Saturday money. That was really a fib I told. I wanted a penknife, you see. But now I am going to spend the whole of my money on that basket for my mother's birthday.'

'Take it with you now,' said the old man, 'and you can bring me the money tomorrow.'

'Will you trust me then?' asked John. 'I told you a fib just now, you know.'

'I'll trust you,' said the old man. 'Go along, little half-and-half. Here's the basket.'

John went, full of wonder and very puzzled. A good many things were suddenly very clear to him. He saw now why it mattered so much whether he chose to do wrong things or right things. He had to make himself, good or bad. The man he was going to be would be exactly as he made him. It was the little things, the right and wrong things he did, that were going to lead to all sorts of big things.

That isn't quite the end of John's story. He's a great doctor now, the kindest and most honest man you could meet. He says that the strange Enchanted Book told him things every child ought to know.

'Most children are half-and-half,' he says. Well, I expect you are too, aren't you? Choose the right half, whatever you do, and let it grow. I can't show you the Enchanted Book, because I don't know where it is now, but if ever I find it, we'll look at it together. I wonder what it will show us!

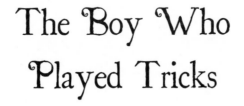

The Boy Who
Played Tricks

The Boy Who
Played Tricks

HARRY YAWNED. He was sitting in class, and he was very bored. *Everyone's working hard, but I can't think of a thing to write down*, he thought. *Maybe if I play a little trick on someone I'll liven things up.*

He wondered what to do. Then he grinned. *I'll hand a note to Jenny – and I'll drop ink all over the other side so that her hand will be covered in black ink!* he thought. *That will make us laugh!*

So he scribbled a note, and then, opening his desk, he hid behind it for a few moments, making blots on the underside of the note with his fountain pen. How wet it was! He left a dry corner to hold it with, and then whispered to Jenny, 'Here – pass this on!'

Jenny held out her hand and took the note. She felt her fingers getting wet, and looked to see why. Oh – how disgusting! The paper was dripping with ink underneath!

The note fell on her dress and made a big mess. Jenny snatched at it and got covered with ink again. She was almost in tears.

Then the bell rang for the end of the lesson. John stood up to hold the door for the teacher to go out. Harry began to laugh loudly, 'Look! Jenny's covered in ink. I handed her a note with ink blots underneath, and—'

'That's a disgusting trick!' said John. 'Look at poor Jenny's dress. Whatever will her mother say?'

'I shall get told off,' said Jenny, with tears in her eyes. 'It was clean on today. You're hateful, Harry!'

'Yes, always playing silly tricks like this,' said Joan. 'You hid all my books the other day and I got into such a row.'

'Well, tricks are funny. They liven us up,' said Harry, still grinning. '*Look* at your hands, Jenny!'

'I've a good mind to wipe the ink on your face,' said Jenny, holding up her hand. Harry dodged at once.

'Making such a fuss about a little trick!' he said crossly. 'It was only meant for fun.'

'Tricks that get other people into trouble aren't funny,' said Peter. 'Your tricks are either silly or unkind. Look how you jump out at people from behind doors – you nearly scared little Fanny out of her wits! Pooh – funny! *That's* not funny!'

'And you took Jane's chair away just as she was going to sit down,' said Doris. 'She hurt her back and couldn't go in for the sports. *That's* not funny either. It's cruel!'

Harry flung himself out of the room. 'Can't stand a few tricks!' he jeered. 'You're a dull lot! I shan't waste my time on you any more.'

'You'd better not,' said John. 'We've had about enough of you. Keep your tricks for home!'

Harry thought he had better! It wasn't nice to have everyone against him like that. Well, he could always play tricks at home! He never played tricks on his father, who was quite stern. But he played plenty on his gentle mother, and on Mrs Brown who came to help with the housework.

He had a store of paper bags. He thought it was really very funny to blow one up, creep behind Mrs Brown and bang the bag with his hand so that it made a loud explosion. Poor Mrs Brown nearly fainted with fright!

He played tricks on his mother too, putting salt in the sugar, and sugar in the salt, so that she really was puzzled at the taste. Harry roared with laughter then.

'But it's such a waste, Harry,' his mother said. 'I have to throw both away. *Please* don't do things like that.'

Now one day Harry saw his mother putting a lot of things into an old wooden box, out in the yard. He watched her, and grinned to himself.

I expect she is collecting things for the jumble sale, he thought. *I'll go and get into the box – it's quite big enough to hold me – and hide there. Next time she takes off the lid I'll pop up and boo! What a shock she'll get!*

He opened the lid. Inside was a lot of rubbish – old hats and clothes and worn-out mats. 'Jumble!' said Harry. He took out the mats to make room for himself, and threw them behind the dustbin. Then he got in and pulled hats and rags over him.

He waited and waited. Nobody came. He thought he would open the lid to give himself a little air. So he pushed at it – but, dear me, it wouldn't open! The clasp had fallen into place, and had clicked shut!

'Blow!' said Harry. 'I hope Mother will come fairly soon. It's terribly stuffy in here!'

He heard footsteps after a moment – not his mother's, but big, heavy ones. Then he suddenly felt himself lifted up high in the air in the box. He yelled in fright. What was happening?

The footsteps walked off, and there was Harry in

the box, high up on somebody's shoulder! He screamed again.

Down the garden path to the back gate. Out into the front garden and out of the front gate. Then the box was flung heavily into something, and Harry felt himself shaken and bumped inside the box. He shouted loudly, 'Let me out! Hey, let me out! I'm in this box!'

Where was he? He was in the dustman's cart! It was the dustman who had walked down the back way to collect the rubbish, and he had taken the box to throw into his cart! Harry's mother had asked him to take it away.

The man went back to get the dustbin. He took that down to the cart and emptied the contents all over the old box. A horrid smell came into the box and Harry yelled again.

But the dustman didn't hear! He had had a bad cold, and his ears were blocked. He didn't hear Harry's screams and shouts; he didn't hear him banging and kicking against the old box!

On went the dustcart, collecting people's rubbish, and all the time Harry yelled and sobbed and hammered on the old box.

Somebody heard him at last. It was John, who happened to be cycling by. He heard the yells and stopped in surprise. Surely they didn't come from the dustcart. But they did!

John called to the dustman, 'I say! There's somebody in your cart. Can't you hear him yelling?'

'What?' asked the dustman. 'Speak up. I can't hear.'

John repeated what he had said, more loudly. The dustman looked most surprised. He began to poke about in the rubbish.

'There's somebody in that big old box!' said John excitedly. 'Look – that one. He's yelling like anything. He must be shut up in it!'

The dustman dragged the box to the top of the rubbish. He undid the fastening – and up came Harry's untidy head! He was sobbing bitterly.

'I couldn't breathe! How dare you take me away? Where am I? What's the horrible smell? OHHHHH! I'm in the dustcart! Let me out, quick!'

The dustman lifted him out. He was roaring with laughter. 'What a joke to tell my pals!' he said. 'My, what a joke! Did somebody play a trick on you, sonny! Ha, ha – I never saw such a funny thing in my life!'

'It isn't a joke! It isn't funny!' wailed poor Harry. 'How dare you! John, please help me home. My legs feel very queer now.'

John helped him home. 'How did you get into the box?' he said. 'Tell me that.'

'No,' said Harry, going red.

'Well, I can guess!' said John. 'One of your silly tricks, of course. You got in there to frighten the person who might be coming to put something into it, didn't you? Your mother perhaps. And the dustman came and took it – and you too. Oh, what a joke! You were playing one of your nasty tricks – and one was

played on you, though the dustman didn't know it –
he can't hear! It serves you right!'

Harry was almost in tears again. 'Don't laugh at
me. It's unkind.'

'I'm only doing what you often do when *you've*
played a trick,' said John. 'Just laughing! Goodness,
what will your mother say when she knows – and all
the boys and girls at school!'

'Don't tell my mother! She might tell my father and
he'd say it served me right,' begged Harry. 'And surely
you wouldn't be so mean as to tell the other children,
John. I'd feel so ashamed.'

'Is there any reason why I shouldn't be mean to
you?' demanded John. 'Haven't you been mean to us
often enough? Now that a wonderful joke has been
played on you, why shouldn't we share it?'

'John, if I promise you never, never to play a
horrid trick again, will you promise not to tell anyone?'
asked Harry, taking hold of John's arm.

John looked at his red, miserable face. 'All right. I

promise – but I shall only keep my promise if you keep yours,' he said. 'So look out!'

Well, so far John has told nobody, so it means that Harry has kept his word. But alas, the dustman didn't keep the joke to himself, so everybody knows what happened to Harry that afternoon. That's how *I* heard about it, of course!

Stand on Your Own Feet

Stand on Your Own Feet

PETER WAS the boy next door. He was eleven years old, strong and jolly and always laughing. Ann liked him very much.

Ann was ten, but was small for her age. People thought she was eight. She was shy and timid, and she was so afraid of being scolded for anything that she never owned up when she was in the wrong.

She sat on the wall and watched Peter shooting arrows at a target. 'Come and have a try!' said Peter, so she slid down and took the big bow.

'Oh dear, it's so big. It won't spring back and hurt me, will it?'

'Aren't you a little coward!' said Peter, laughing. 'Of course it won't. Look – do it like this.'

It was fun playing with Peter. They took turns at shooting arrows at the target, and then suddenly Ann shot one that went right over the wall! There was a loud 'miaow' and the next-door cat leapt high in the air. The arrow had hit it!

'Oh! Poor thing!' said Peter, and he was over the wall in a flash. But the cat, full of terror, ran away limping. Peter knew he couldn't catch it. He went back over the wall.

'We'd better go round and knock at Miss Milner's door and tell her you hit the cat by accident,' said Peter.

Ann stared at him in the greatest alarm. What! Go and own up to old Miss Milner, who had a very cross face indeed? Why, she wouldn't know a thing about the cat if nobody told her. So why tell her?

'We don't need to say *anything*,' said Ann. 'She would never know it was one of our arrows that hit her cat. And I don't expect the cat's hurt much, anyway. Miss Milner is *terribly* fierce, you know.'

Peter looked fierce too, quite suddenly. He stared scornfully at Ann. 'Do you know what you are? You're a cowardy custard! Afraid of owning up! The cat *might* be badly hurt – we don't know – and we ought to tell about it. We didn't do it on purpose. Miss Milner will know it was an accident.'

'Oh, but, Peter, she'll be so *cross*,' said Ann, her eyes filling with tears.

'And what does that matter?' said Peter still in his horrid, scornful voice. 'Have people never been cross with you? Why shouldn't they be sometimes? I feel very cross with you myself. I know it's horrid when people are cross, but even if we don't like it we needn't be *afraid* of it.'

'You come with me then, Peter,' wept Ann. '*You* tell Miss Milner. And oh, couldn't you say it was *your* arrow that hit the cat? I always feel so scared when things like this happen. You're big and brave, and you're a boy. I'm a girl, and Mummy says I'm timid and sensitive.'

'Timid and sensitive!' said Peter sneeringly. 'That's what people often say when their children are cowardly and deceitful. Pooh! You're only a year younger than I am, and what does it matter if you're a girl? I've got a cousin of nine called Jean – and she's as brave as anything. She's coming to stay soon, and I'll be glad to have her. She can stand on her own feet – *you* always want to stand on somebody else's.'

'I don't, I don't,' sobbed Ann, thinking that Peter was very unkind.

'You do,' said Peter. 'When you got into trouble at school you asked your mother to put it right for you instead of taking your punishment properly. And when you broke Lucy's ruler in half you were afraid to tell her. You got George to explain about it to Lucy. And now you want *me* to go and tell Miss Milner that *I* shot the arrow at the cat. Why can't you stand on your own feet?'

Ann didn't answer. She wiped her eyes and sniffed.

'You'll grow up into a milk-and-water, namby-pamby, weak and silly person,' went on Peter. 'My mother says people like that have never learnt to stand on their own feet and face up to things.'

Ann began to cry again. 'You don't like me! You won't want to play with me any more.'

Peter looked at Ann and felt sorry for her – but not *too* sorry! No, that would never do. He took her arm and shook it gently.

'Ann! I'm going to tell you something nice now. I do like you. You're fun to play with, and if you'd be brave and stand on your own feet *always*, I'd like you as much as I like anyone. But if you don't stand on your own feet I shan't be friends with you at all. You won't be worth it!'

Ann sniffed again, then wiped her eyes and put away her hanky. She looked at Peter, so straight and tall and fearless. She would never, never be like him – but she could at least *try*. She didn't want him to think Jean was wonderful and play only with her when she came to stay with him. It would be horrid to be left out because she was feeble and silly and a coward.

'I think you've said worse things than any grown-up would say,' she told him. 'But I think perhaps you're right. I don't believe I ever do stand on my own feet. You watch me now!'

And to Peter's enormous surprise she went out of his garden and up the front path to Miss Milner's house, where she knocked on the door.

When she heard footsteps along the hallway inside she almost ran away. This was the very first time Ann had ever owned up to anything by herself, and although she had felt very brave when she had spoken to Peter, she didn't feel at all brave now.

The door opened – and there stood the cross-faced Miss Milner. 'What do you want?' she said.

Ann could hardly get the words out, she was so afraid. 'Please – quite by accident – I hit your cat with an arrow. I thought I'd better tell you, in case she was hurt. I'm so sorry.'

Ann stammered all this out with a very red face, and then turned to run away. But Miss Milner caught hold of her arm.

'Wait!' she said. 'Let's have a look at the cat. She's in the kitchen. How *nice* of you to tell me. Most children wouldn't have said a word.'

Ann's heart was still beating fast as she went with Miss Milner into her kitchen. The cat was there in front of the fire. Miss Milner examined her.

'She has a little lump on this leg, but that's all,' she said. 'I don't think she's hurt much. Thank you for telling me. I think a lot of you for that – and when I see your mother I shall tell her what a brave little girl she's got, to come and own up like this.'

'Peter made me,' said Ann, going red again. 'I was afraid to.'

'Well, here are biscuits for you both,' said Miss Milner, reaching up for a tin. 'I made them myself.

That boy Peter is a good lad – absolutely trustworthy. He'll make a fine man, there's no doubt about that!'

She gave Ann the biscuits and smiled at her. Ann was astonished. Why, Miss Milner hadn't a cross face after all! She thanked her and raced back to Peter, her face glowing. They munched the biscuits together while Ann told all that had happened.

'There you are, you see – as soon as you stand on your own feet things aren't nearly so frightening as you think,' said Peter. 'But, mind you, even if they *are* frightening it's still no reason for not facing up to them. I must say I never thought you had it in you, Ann, to own up like that!'

Ann thought about many things that night in bed. She remembered a lot too. She remembered how she had once broken one of the panes in the garden shed and hadn't owned up, and Daddy thought it was the odd-job boy who had done it. She remembered how she had got into trouble at school over forgotten homework, and had begged her mother to go and tell her teacher she hadn't been well and that was why the work wasn't done. And, oh, dear, Mother had done what Ann wanted; perhaps Mother didn't know it was wrong not to let her stand on her own feet.

Ann remembered other things. Mother was always making excuses for her. She wouldn't let Daddy scold her when she had broken his fountain pen. She wouldn't let Granny be cross with her when Ann had left the tap running in the basin and flooded the floor. She hadn't even made Ann go and tell Granny herself – Mother had gone to tell her and explain.

I've been standing on other people's feet for ages, thought Ann, feeling ashamed. *It's going to be hard to stand on my own now. I hope they'll bear my weight!*

That made her smile. She thought of Peter. However afraid he might be, he always seemed strong and brave and sensible. She wanted him to think well of her. She fell asleep making up her mind that she would be far, far better than his wonderful cousin Jean!

Well, it wasn't easy to keep her word to Peter. All kinds of things happened that seemed to make things as difficult as possible.

She lost one of her exercise books on the way to school, and because she knew she would have to stay in at playtime and get a few sharp words from her teacher she simply could *not* tell her.

She kept thinking what to say and then not saying it. In despair she went to Peter between lessons and told him. 'I'm a coward after all,' she said. 'I simply *can't* own up!'

'Now you go straight away this minute and say, "Miss Brown, I'm sorry. I must have dropped my exercise book on the way to school",' said Peter. 'Go on. This very minute. The more you think of it the worse it will be. It's best to do these things *at once.*'

Peter was right, of course. It was always best to face up to things at once and get them over. Miss Brown wasn't even cross! She put her hand into her desk –

and brought out Ann's exercise book. 'Here it is,' she said. 'Somebody picked it up and brought it to me. Put your name in it, you know that's the rule.'

Ann felt so relieved. How silly she had been to worry herself all the morning! If only she had gone to Miss Brown at once.

The next day she broke one of Mother's vases. Ann was horrified. Still, she knew how to get round Mother. She would wait till Mother found the vase, then she would say she had meant to tell her, and she would cry – and Mother wouldn't scold at all!

'You coward!' Ann said to herself when she had thought all this. 'Horrid, deceitful little coward! Go at once and tell Mother.'

And she went. Mother was upset, and told Ann she was careless.

'Yes,' said Ann. 'I *was* careless. Let me buy you another vase out of my own money, Mother.'

That made Mother feel very pleased. Ann suddenly felt pleased herself. How nice it was to stand on your own feet! You really did think more of yourself. She felt quite ten feet taller!

Then Daddy was quite cross because Ann had left her bicycle out in the rain. Usually she would have run to Mother and cried and asked her to tell Daddy she hadn't meant to – but not this time.

'Daddy, I'm sorry,' she said. 'I absolutely forgot my bike. I'll dry it and clean it this evening. It won't happen again.'

Her father looked at her in surprise. Usually Ann wept buckets of tears, and made all kinds of excuses. This was a new Ann, an Ann he liked very much.

'Spoken like a brave lass!' he said, and Ann went red with pleasure.

Still, things weren't easy at all, because it does take a long time to learn to stand on your own feet when you've been using someone else's for ten years! Ann was often afraid, often quite in despair when things went wrong, and she had to somehow summon up enough courage to face them all by herself. She was determined not to ask Mother or Daddy or Peter to help her in anything. It must be her own feet she stood on and nobody else's!

Everyone noticed the change in Ann. Only Peter understood it. He was pleased and proud. Proud of himself because he had made Ann into a nicer person, and proud of Ann for being able to find courage to do it.

And then, just before Peter's cousin Jean was due to arrive, something else happened. Ann was out on her bicycle, riding some way behind a small boy. Suddenly a dog ran out and collided with the back wheel of the boy's bicycle. Off he fell at once and lay in the road, squealing with fright and pain.

And what did Ann do? She didn't do what she would have done three weeks before – screamed and ridden away as fast as she could.

No, she rode up to the boy, shooed away the big playful dog, helped up the screaming child and took him into the nearest house to have his cut knees seen to. She found out his name and address and went riding off to tell his mother and to ask her to come and fetch him home.

Peter heard about it because the boy's mother was a great friend of his own mother's, and told her all about Ann. 'A more sensible, helpful child I never saw!' said the little boy's mother. 'Stood on her own feet, and did all the right things at once. Now, I do like a child like that.'

Peter was bursting with pride. He rushed off to tell Ann. She went red and looked away. She was so pleased to hear Peter's praise that she couldn't say a word.

'I'm glad you're my friend,' said Peter. 'You really are a friend to be proud of.'

'It's a pity Jean's coming tomorrow,' said Ann with a sigh. 'Just as I'm getting sensible enough to be your friend. Now you'll have Jean and you won't want anyone else to play with.'

'Jean will like you awfully,' said Peter. 'Come and

play every day, will you? We'll go for picnics together and go swimming. It'll be fun, the three of us.'

It *is* fun. Ann's having a lovely time. She always stands on her own feet now, and what I would dearly like to know is – do you?

Boastful Bill

Boastful Bill

BILL WAS a big boy. He was only eight years old, but he was tall for his age, and everyone thought he was ten. He liked people to think that. He boasted that he could do this, that and the other – he could ride ten miles straight off on his bicycle and not feel tired, he could swim eight times up and down the school baths, he could row a boat across the river and back and not stop once. Oh, Bill was a wonderful chap – if you listened to him!

Next door to Bill lived the twins, Mollie and John. They were seven years old and small for their age. They had no bicycles, so when Bill boasted about his riding, they thought him very wonderful indeed. They had never been in a boat, so they couldn't row. How marvellous Bill must be to row across the river all by himself!

'All the same, I don't much like Bill, although he's so clever and wonderful,' said Mollie to John. 'He never seems to think anyone else can do anything. I know we are small for our age and can't do anything much, but I do get a bit tired of hearing all the things Bill can do!'

When the summer holidays came Bill asked John and Mollie where they were going.

'We are going to Seasands,' said Mollie.

'How funny! So am I!' said Bill. 'My word, we shall be able to have some fine times together. We have a boat, and a beach hut and a floating bed that you blow up and lie on. Last year I had great fun on that – can't tell you how many people I pushed off it into the water! My word, they did swallow a lot of salty water too!'

Mollie and John looked at one another. It wouldn't be much fun to be pushed off the floating bed too often. They were so small, and Bill was so big! Bill could push them off each time, but they were quite sure they wouldn't be able to push him off at all!

The seaside holidays came at last. Mollie and John went down to Seasands with their father and mother. They were so excited about it!

The first person they saw on the beach when they got there was Bill, of course. There he was, sitting in a boat, looking as if the whole place belonged to him.

'Hallo!' he said. 'I've just been for a row all round the bay.'

Mollie looked at the boat. It seemed very dry outside, not at all as if it had been in the water. But she was too polite to say anything.

'I've bathed twice already today,' said Bill. 'The water was jolly cold too! I didn't feel warm till I'd swum right out to that rock over there!'

Mollie and John looked at the rock. It seemed very

far away indeed. They thought Bill must be a fine swimmer to swim so far.

'We can swim too,' said John. 'But not so far as that.'

'Pooh! Little shrimps like you can't do much,' said Bill. 'I say! What about building a whopping big castle, the biggest ever made? We've plenty of time before the tide comes in. We'll have towers on it and a tunnel right through – and bits of glass from the beach for the windows!'

So they began to build the big castle. Mollie and John worked hard, but Bill didn't seem to do much except tell them how to make the towers, and pat the sand here and there to make it smooth, and find bits of glass and seaweed to decorate the castle.

It wasn't very big after all. Bill said it was because Mollie and John weren't big or strong enough to dig as he could. Mollie thought he hadn't dug much, but she didn't like to say so.

'What about a bathe?' said John, who was longing to go into the calm blue water. 'I'd like that.'

'Yes, that would be fun,' said Mollie. 'Have you got that floating bed you talked about, Bill?'

'Yes, it's in our beach hut,' said Bill, but he didn't seem to want to fetch it. So Mollie went to the hut and got it out. It certainly was a fine bed. It was blown up and full of air, all ready to take out on the sea. What fun! Mollie hoped she wouldn't be pushed off too often.

Soon they were all in bathing suits. Mollie and John had theirs under their clothes, so they didn't take long to get ready. They waited for Bill, who was in the hut. He came out at last.

'Let's run straight in and dive under a big wave,' said John. He and Mollie raced into the sea, and threw themselves under a big green curling wave. Oh, how lovely! The water felt cold at first, but the children were soon warm with swimming.

Bill didn't dive in as they had done. He stood up to his knees – and he shivered! Mollie couldn't help laughing. 'Come on, Bill!' she called. 'It's lovely. You said you had already been in twice, and it must have been colder earlier in the day. It's warm now.'

Bill went a little further – and a bit further. Really, if Mollie and John hadn't known he was a fine swimmer they would have thought he was just a baby! At last he was in. He made a great show of splashing about, but he didn't go out very far.

'Come on out here,' called John, who was quite enjoying himself in deep water. 'You can't feel the bottom out here.'

'I'm going to lie on the bed,' said Bill. He fetched the red floating bed and lay on it. Then he called Mollie and said she could have a turn, but no sooner was she on than he tipped her off, splash!

Then John climbed on and Bill tipped him off too, splash! But nobody could tip Bill off – he was too big and heavy.

'It's cold if we don't swim about,' said Molly. 'Come on, John, let Bill float about if he wants to. We'll go for a swim.'

So off they went. Billy lay down on the bed, shut his eyes and let himself float up and down on the waves. The sun was warm on the bed. Bill fell asleep. He didn't hear Mollie and John yelling to him. He didn't wake up for fifteen minutes, and by that time the bed had floated almost to the big rock that Bill had pointed to so proudly when he had told Mollie and John that he had swum there and back.

Bill sat up in a fright. He stared around at the sea. Ooh! He had floated out ever so far! He would never be able to swim back! Oh, he would be drowned! Oh, he would float to America! He would – he would! Bill burst into tears and yelled for help.

'Swim back, silly, swim back!' shouted Mollie and John. 'You said you could swim as far as that rock this morning. Go on, jump in and swim.'

But Bill didn't. He sat and wept loudly on the bed.

'I say, Mollie, I don't believe the silly chap was speaking the truth when he said he was such a fine swimmer,' said John suddenly. 'You know what a baby he was about getting into the water – well, no good swimmer does that sort of thing. I think he was just boasting. What shall we do?'

'John, you swim after the bed, and see if you can get hold of it and guide it towards that rock,' said Mollie. 'I'll get the boat that Bill was in and row after you. I can get to the rock, I think, and we'll all row back.'

'Can you manage the boat, Mollie?' said John, swimming off. 'You've never tried a boat before, you know.'

'I've seen other people do it,' said Mollie. 'I'll be all right. Go on after Bill, quickly.'

So John swam hard after the floating bed. He caught it at last and then swam to the rock, pushing the bed in front of him. Bill sat and howled on the bed. He wouldn't jump out into the water and help John. He just behaved like a silly baby.

John managed to get to the rock that stuck up out of the water. He sat on it, panting. Bill got off the bed and sat on the rock too. John dragged the bed up to them. He soon got his breath and turned to look at Bill, whose eyes were all red with crying.

'Why didn't you jump off the bed and swim to shore with it when you saw you were floating out?' asked John.

'I can't swim so far,' said Bill sulkily, going red.

'Then you are a silly boaster,' said John. 'And a baby besides. Fancy howling like this! For goodness' sake, stop before Mollie comes. Look at her, bringing that boat out all by herself to rescue us. She's never been in a boat before, but she's rowing as well as a sailor could!'

So she was! She was pulling at the oars well, and although she was small, she managed that boat beautifully. She reached the rock at last and the two boys got in.

'Now you take the oars and row back, Bill,' said John. 'Mollie's tired, and so am I. She's had a long row, and I've had a long swim. You've only had a good long float.'

'I can't row as far as that,' said Bill, redder than ever. Mollie and John stared at him in amazement.

'Well, you jolly well row as far as you can,' said John. 'Lazy creature! Go on, take the oars and row! If you think Mollie or I are going to row you back all the way, you're wrong. We may rest here for a while and swim back ourselves. You can have the boat!'

'Oh, no, John, oh, no!' said Bill, beginning to cry again. 'Don't do that. I'll row as best I can.'

So he took the oars and began. But he couldn't row a bit! The boat hardly moved at all!

In the end John took the oars and rowed them back to shore. And there, waiting for them, was Bill's father.

'Well, young man,' he said sternly to Bill, 'you've made a fine baby of yourself this morning, haven't you? Had to have this youngster swimming after you to get you and the bed – and this little girl to fetch you in a boat – and then you couldn't even row back! And you've had the boat for three years now!'

Bill stood on the sand looking very small indeed, although he was such a big chap. Mollie and John stared at him in surprise and disgust, remembering the wonderful tales he had told them of the things he could do.

'Come along in and get your lunch now,' said Bill's father. 'As for the bed and the boat, these children shall have them for themselves while they are down here. It is quite clear that you are not big enough to use them!'

Bill went home. So did Mollie and John.

'I say, it's fun to have a boat and that bed to use!' said Mollie gleefully. 'But I'm sorry for Bill. He was awfully silly.'

'Let's be decent to him,' said John. 'We won't say a single word to him about today, but in future, Mollie, he's got to do as *we* tell him, and if he begins to boast we'll just laugh – and laugh and laugh!'

So now Bill doesn't boast any more and is very much nicer. He can swim much better, and since

Mollie and John have made him take his turn at the oars, he rows quite well too. It *is* silly to boast, isn't it? – especially when you can't do what you're boasting about!

Acknowledgements

All efforts have been made to seek necessary permissions.

The stories in this publication first appeared in the following publications:

'Untidy William' first appeared in *Enid Blyton's Sunny Stories*, Nos. 255 and 256, 1941.

'She Stamped Her Foot' first appeared in *Enid Blyton's Sunny Stories*, No. 197, 1940.

'He Was a Bit Too Quick!' first appeared in *Enid Blyton's Sunny Stories*, No. 448, 1949.

'The Poisonous Berries' first appeared in *Enid Blyton's Sunny Stories*, No. 144, 1939.

'Billy Bitten-Nails' first appeared in *Enid Blyton's Sunny Stories*, No. 61, 1938.

'The Forgotten Canary' first appeared in *Enid Blyton's Sunny Stories*, No. 173, 1940.

'Fussy Philip' first appeared as 'Fussy Philip!' in *Enid Blyton's Sunny Stories*, Nos. 284 and 285, 1942.

'The Magic Hummybugs' first appeared in *Enid Blyton's Sunny Stories*, No. 88, 1938.

'A Little Thing that Made a Big Thing' first appeared in *A Book of Naughty Children*, published by Methuen in 1944.

'Polly's P's and Q's' first appeared in *Enid Blyton's Sunny Stories*, No. 175, 1940.

'The Dirty Little Boy' first appeared in *Sunny Stories for Little Folks*, No. 244, 1936.

'Sulky Susan' first appeared in *Enid Blyton's Sunny Stories*, No. 235, 1941.

'The Magic Biscuits' first appeared in *Enid Blyton's Sunny Stories*, No. 26, 1937.

'The Boy Who Made Faces' first appeared in *Enid Blyton's Sunny Stories*, No. 435, 1948.

'The Tell-Tale Bird' first appeared in *Enid Blyton's Sunny Stories*, No. 98, 1938.

'Porridge Town' first appeared in *Enid Blyton's Sunny Stories*, No. 232, 1941.

'Sally's Silly Mistake' first appeared as 'Sally Simple's Mistake' in *Enid Blyton's Sunny Stories*, No. 455, 1949.

'The Astonishing Party' first appeared in *Enid Blyton's Sunny Stories*, No. 351, 1945.

'The Boy Who Was Too Clever' first appeared in *Enid Blyton's Sunny Stories*, No. 37, 1937.

'A Shock for Lucy Ann!' first appeared in *Enid Blyton's Sunny Stories*, No. 30, 1937.

'He Was Afraid!' first appeared in *Enid Blyton's Sunny Stories*, No. 430, 1948.

'Mummy's New Scissors' first appeared in *Enid Blyton's Sunny Stories*, No. 492, 1950.

'The Very Funny Tail' first appeared in *Enid Blyton's Sunny Stories*, No. 220, 1941.

'The Girl Who Tore Her Books' first appeared in *Enid Blyton's Sunny Stories*, No. 8, 1937.

'The Naughty Little Storyteller' first appeared as 'The Naughty Little Story-Teller' in *Enid Blyton's Sunny Stories*, No. 13, 1937.

'A Story of Tidiness and Untidiness' first appeared in *The Adventurous Duck and other Stories*, published by Parragon in 1997.

'The Enchanted Book' first appeared in *Enid Blyton's Sunny Stories*, No. 305, 1943.

'The Boy Who Played Tricks' first appeared in *Enid Blyton's Magazine*, No. 2, Vol. 1, 1953.

'Stand on Your Own Feet' first appeared as 'Stand On Your Own Feet!' in *Enid Blyton's Sunny Stories*, No. 449, 1949.

'Boastful Bill' first appeared in *Enid Blyton's Sunny Stories*, No. 27, 1937.

Enid Blyton

Look out for these enchanting
short-story collections…

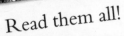

Read them all!

ENIDBLYTON.CO.UK
IS FOR PARENTS, CHILDREN AND TEACHERS!

Sign up to the newsletter on the homepage for a monthly round-up of news from the world of

Enid Blyton

Enid Blyton

is one of the most popular children's authors of all time.
Her books have sold over 500 million copies and have
been translated into other languages more often than
any other children's author.

Enid Blyton adored writing for children. She wrote over
700 books and about 2,000 short stories. *The Famous Five*
books, now 75 years old, are her most popular. She is also
the author of other favourites including *The Secret Seven*,
The Magic Faraway Tree, *Malory Towers* and *Noddy*.

Born in London in 1897, Enid lived much of her life
in Buckinghamshire and loved dogs, gardening and the
countryside. She was very knowledgeable about trees,
flowers, birds and animals.

Dorset – where some
of the Famous Five's
adventures are set –
was a favourite place
of hers too.

Enid Blyton's
stories are read
and loved by
millions of children
(and grown-ups)
all over the world.
Visit enidblyton.co.uk
to discover more.